"I Intend to Take You Seriously, Maggie."

His voice was low, silky, seductive, his heavy-lidded gaze burning with unspoken promise. "In fact, I'll take you any way I can get you."

"Oh!" Maggie gasped, her eyes wide. "Oh, you . . . you . . ." To her utter dismay, she felt her body respond to the husky sensuality in his words. Held captive by the sexual tension that crackled in the air between them, she trembled with a confusing, frustrating mixture of excitement and anger.

Damn the man! She was perfectly happy as she was. When and if she wanted another man in her life, it wouldn't be the likes of Clinton Rafferty. She wasn't *that* much of a fool.

GINNA GRAY

admits that for most of her life she has been both an avid reader and a dreamer. For a long time the desire to write, to put her fantasies down on paper, had been growing, until finally she told herself to *do* it. Now she can't imagine *not* writing.

Dear Reader:

I'd like to take this opportunity to thank you for all your support and encouragement of Silhouette Romances.

Many of you write in regularly, telling us what you like best about Silhouette, which authors are your favorites. This is a tremendous help to us as we strive to publish the best contemporary romances possible.

All the romances from Silhouette Books are for you, so enjoy this book and the many stories to come.

Karen Solem
Editor-in-Chief
Silhouette Books

GINNA GRAY
The Perfect Match

Silhouette *Romance*

Published by Silhouette Books New York

America's Publisher of Contemporary Romance

Silhouette Books by Ginna Gray

The Gentling (ROM #285)
Golden Illusion (SE #171)
The Perfect Match (ROM #311)

SILHOUETTE BOOKS, a Division of Simon & Schuster, Inc.
1230 Avenue of the Americas, New York, N.Y. 10020

ISBN: 0-671-57311-X

First Silhouette Books printing August, 1984

10 9 8 7 6 5 4 3 2 1

Map by Ray Lundgren

America's Publisher of Contemporary Romance

Printed in the U.S.A.

BC91

To my mother, Ruby Conn, for her loving encouragement and support

The Perfect Match

TEXAS

Chapter One

Standing in the shadows to one side of the set, amid the snaking cables and cords that covered the studio floor, Maggie Trent waited impatiently for the show's wrap-up, her eyes flicking back and forth between the live action and the viewing monitor a few feet away. The director switched to the wide-angle perspective of camera two, bringing all the guests into the final shot. Alex very politely thanked each one in turn for appearing, but Maggie noticed the way his eyes kept returning to the voluptuous young actress. Maggie shook her head, laughing softly. Men! They were all the same.

"This portion of 'Houston Today,' with host Alex Crenna, has been brought to you by Sporting Chance, the Southwest's quality sporting goods stores," announced Harvey Goodman in his most mellifluous tones while the credits flashed across the screen.

A moment later Maggie's own name appeared, and

after it that of the show's director. Then followed the momentary fade-out into commercial. Maggie picked her briefcase up from the floor and started forward.

"Alex, could I speak with you for a moment?"

Alex broke off his conversation with the young starlet at once. "Sure thing, Maggie. Be right with you." Hurriedly he thanked his guests once again and, after one last, regretful glance at the blonde, excused himself and strode over to where Maggie stood waiting.

"What's up, boss lady?" His handsome face split into a dazzling white smile.

"I just had a call from Henry Burk," Maggie replied in a clipped voice that sobered him instantly. "He wants us to have lunch with him and his new partner on Monday. So if you have anything else on tap you'd better cancel it."

Alex's blond brows rose. "Henry has taken on a *partner?*"

"Apparently so. And while he didn't come right out and say it, I got the impression that the new man isn't all that sold on sponsoring the show."

"Who is this partner? And why would Henry bring someone else into the business when the Sporting Chance stores are doing so well? He has branches all over the Gulf Coast area and is expanding all the time."

"I don't know the answers to any of those questions," Maggie admitted with a shrug. "All Henry would tell me was that the man's a well-known sports figure. It seems they're keeping the whole deal hush-hush until they're ready to release the news to the press. In any case, it's fairly obvious that we're going to have to do a selling job. Their contract with us comes up for renewal next month. If we lose Henry the show will go off the air, unless we can hustle up another major sponsor on short notice."

Alex ran an agitated hand through his expertly styled

golden hair. "You know I'll do whatever I can to help," he assured her in a concerned tone that brought a smile back to Maggie's lips.

Though Alex viewed his role as host of Houston's most popular local talk show merely as a stepping stone, he knew very well it was an important stepping stone. If the show were dropped his chances of advancing to a major network job on the East Coast were nil. Maggie knew she could count on his help.

"Selene will be there also, since her agency is handling all the publicity for Sporting Chance. She'll give us whatever support she can. I think, among the three of us, we'll be able to persuade him." Maggie slipped into the cream suit jacket she'd been carrying, adjusted the collar of her red silk blouse over the lapels, then turned and headed for the exit. "But for now, I intend to put Henry and his new partner out of my mind and enjoy a relaxing weekend. This has been one lulu of a week, and I'm bushed."

Alex fell in step beside her. "In that case, I don't suppose I could talk you into dinner and a bit of dancing afterward, could I?"

A sardonic smile curved Maggie's mouth. She glanced over her shoulder at the sexy blonde and raised one brow. "I'm surprised you didn't ask Miss Harper."

"Now why on earth would I do that? I much prefer a certain feisty, blue-eyed brunette."

Maggie gave him a dry look that spoke volumes. "Struck out, did you?"

"Hell, I didn't even get up to bat," Alex admitted, cheerfully unabashed. "Seems Miss Harper is flying back to Hollywood tonight."

"Ah, well, you can't win 'em all."

"True. But I'd think the least you could do is console me. After all, what are friends for?"

The woebegone look on his handsome face drew a

chuckle from Maggie. Since her divorce from Larry, she and Alex had dated casually, and their relationship was a comfortable one. They were, indeed, friends. Nothing more. Alex was too wrapped up in his career and his plans for the future to have room in his life for a woman, and Maggie had been burned too badly to want any sort of emotional involvement. While she knew that Alex would not have been averse to having a purely physical affair, he didn't push it. He was far too shrewd to offend the producer of his show.

"Sorry. Not tonight. I couldn't even if I had the energy. Laura's new friend Allison is spending the weekend."

"Surely it's safe to leave two thirteen year olds on their own for a few hours," Alex argued persuasively.

"True, but all the same, I think I'd better stay home with them. I got the feeling from talking to Mr. Rafferty on the phone that he is a very protective father. I'm not sure he would approve of me leaving the girls alone to go out on a date."

"Maybe we can make it next week sometime," she said placatingly, as Alex held the door open for her. "Right now I have to make a quick trip to the grocery store before I pick up Laura and Allison. You'd be amazed at how much food two thirteen-year-old girls can put away in a weekend.

Laura Trent flopped down onto the padded bench in the lobby of Miss Ludmilla Brovnic's Dance Academy and stared at her friend in faint alarm. "Oh, Allison, I don't think that's a very good idea," she croaked.

"Nonsense. My father and your mother are perfect for each other." A bead of perspiration escaped Allison Rafferty's black ponytailed hair and trickled down the side of her face. She picked up the end of the towel looped around her neck and wiped the trickle away, then propped a foot on the bench and began to unlace the ribbon ties on her ballet slippers. "All we have to do is get them together."

"You don't understand," Laura wailed. "If my mother ever finds out we set the whole thing up, she'll kill me!"

"She won't find out. Just leave everything to me. I'll be very subtle about it."

"But you told me yourself your father isn't interested in getting married again. Why should he, when he dates all those beautiful girls? And I *know* my mother isn't," Laura insisted.

"Look, my father dates those girls for just two reasons. Mainly because they're safe."

"Safe?"

"Yeah. Not one of them is the type of woman he'd be even remotely interested in marrying, so he doesn't have to worry about being tempted."

"What's the other reason?"

Allison tilted her head and gave her a disgusted look. "Come on, Laura. You're not *that* dumb," she drawled, rolling her eyes heavenward.

Reddening, Laura ducked her head and whispered a soft, "Oh."

"Anyway, once they get to know each other they'll both change their minds about marriage," Allison declared confidently. "You'll see."

"Gee, I don't know. What if . . ."

"Don't worry." Allison sat down on the bench and grasped her friend's hands. "Laura, your mom is super. She's just the kind of woman my dad should marry, even if he doesn't know it." She gave Laura's hands a squeeze and grinned. "And just think, if we do get them married to each other, you and I will be sisters. We'll be a family."

Glancing out the window, her face softened.

"There's your mom now," Allison said in a low, almost reverent tone. "Gee, just look at her. She's something else, isn't she."

Unaware of being watched, Maggie strode confidently toward the dancing school entrance, the pleated skirt of her cream suit swirling around her shapely legs, her face lifted to the last dwindling rays of the sun. Her eyes sparkled, and a beguiling smile curved her mouth as she breathed in deeply to savor the subtle tang of fall in the air. With every jaunty step her shoulder-length, mahogany hair, parted just slightly off center and curving under around her jaw and neck, swung like a shining brown bell. The two men standing in front of the shop next to the dance school stopped their conversation and smiled appreciatively as she walked by.

Maggie noted their reaction but was neither offended nor flattered. At thirty-three she had long ago come to terms with her looks and knew she was attractive. When she had been younger she had longed to be beautiful and glamorous, but a too wide mouth, large blue eyes, and a slightly turned up nose that even now was sprinkled with freckles in the summer had given her oval face a fresh, wholesome beauty, a "girl next door" prettiness. If she harbored any lingering dissatisfaction about herself it was due to her size. Maggie had always longed to be tall and willowy, one of those sophisticated model types who looks terrific in just any old rag. Instead she was stuck with a petite, curvy body.

Just as Maggie reached the school entrance, Laura and Allison stepped outside, each wearing a wraparound skirt over her leotard and tights and carrying a ballet bag filled with slippers, toe shoes, leg warmers, towels, and assorted other paraphernalia.

"Hi, girls," Maggie greeted, leaning over to give her daughter a quick kiss on the cheek and absently tuck a loose strand of brown hair behind her ear. "Are you two ready for your big weekend?"

"Sure, Mom."

"You bet, Mrs. Trent. Except that . . ." Pausing, Allison bit her lower lip and gave Maggie a doubtful look, her eyes wide and appealing. "Well, you see . . . I forgot to bring my skates, and I was sorta wondering if you could take me by my house so I could pick them up? I'd call my dad to bring them over to me, but he's going out on a date tonight."

Maggie placed an arm around each girl's shoulders, turning them toward the car on the other side of the parking lot. "Of course I will. It's not out of the way, and it will only take a minute."

During the short drive the two girls chattered away nonstop. Maggie was pleased by the friendship that had developed between them. Laura had always tended to be rather shy and withdrawn, and exposure to Allison's sparkling personality had been good for her. Lately Laura showed definite signs of coming out of her shell.

The girls had met only a few weeks ago at the beginning of school, but already they were fast friends. Maggie had learned from Allison that her mother had died five years before and she and her father had just recently moved to Houston from San Antonio.

She hadn't met Mr. Rafferty yet, but during their talks over the phone he had seemed quite amiable. Certainly he had seemed a loving and concerned parent, judging from the third degree he had put her through before agreeing to allow Allison to spend the weekend.

When they pulled into the Rafferty drive the pillared, two-storied colonial home was in darkness. Allison's touching show of fear over entering the house alone was all the persuasion it took for Maggie to agree to accompany her.

Allison let them in with her key and turned on the dim foyer light, then moved toward the arched opening on the right. Maggie and Laura followed automatically. Groping along the wall, Allison located the switch and flipped it up. Immediately the room was flooded with light.

"What in the name of hell!"

The muffled exclamation drew three pair of rounded eyes to the sofa just as a couple scrambled up from its depths in a tangle of arms and legs.

Gaining his feet, the man whirled to face the trio of female intruders. When he spied Allison, his face was at first thunderstruck, then livid.

"Allison! What the devil are you doing here? You're suppose to be spending the night with your friend."

"I am . . . I was . . . I mean . . ." She waved vaguely at Maggie. "This is Laura's mother, Mrs. Trent."

For just an instant the man looked embarrassed, a faint flush running up beneath his tanned skin, but then his face tightened and blazing green eyes leveled on Maggie like twin laser beams. "I see. Then may I ask exactly what it is you're doing here, Mrs. Trent? Or do you make it a habit to barge into a person's home unannounced?"

Maggie stared. This . . . this *hunk* was Allison's *father?* Never in her entire life had she seen a more rawly masculine man. Broad-shouldered, narrow-hipped, and positively oozing sex appeal, he towered over her five-foot-two frame by more than a foot. Somewhere in his mid- to late thirties, and evidently in superb physical shape, he was a stunning example of a man in his prime. When Maggie's gaze locked on heavy-lidded, breathtakingly sexy green eyes staring demandingly at her from beneath thick, dark brows, her heart executed a funny little skip. To avoid that disconcertingly direct look, she quickly lowered her eyes, but when they came to rest on firm, sensual lips her erratic pulse missed another beat.

"I . . . uh . . . that is . . ."

"I'm waiting for an explanation, Mrs. Trent."

"Daddy!" Allison interceded, scandalized. "I can't believe you're talking to Mrs. Trent this way! It's hardly her fault you got caught making out on the couch."

His attention switched immediately to Allison. "Now see here, young lady . . ."

Maggie was so struck by the man's overwhelming presence she was barely aware of the heated discussion that flared between father and daughter. Dazed and utterly fascinated, she continued her inspection.

Clinton Rafferty's face had a bony, chiseled look that just saved it from being too handsome, the cheekbones sharp, the jaw square and thrusting. The bold blade of a nose bore a telltale bump on its bridge that gave mute testimony to the fact that it had been broken, at least once. Fanning out from the corners of his eyes was a network of tiny lines that Maggie knew would crinkle attractively when he smiled. All in all, he was the most attractive, virile-looking man she had ever seen.

And the angriest.

Snapping out of her daze, Maggie stepped to Allison's side. "Allison, dear, don't worry about it. I can understand perfectly why your father is upset." She paused and slanted the furious man a look that was brimming with scornful amusement. Why was it, she wondered, that people tended to react with defensive anger when caught in an embarrassing situation? "If our positions were reversed I'm sure I'd feel the same," she assured the girl gently. Privately, Maggie couldn't conceive of ever finding herself in such a position, and she was quite certain her expression told him as much.

When his nostrils began to flare, Maggie forced a conciliatory smile to her lips and added pleasantly, "I really am sorry we walked in at such an . . . uh . . . inconvenient time, but you see, Allison forgot her skates."

She bit back a smile as she watched him absorb this bit of information and struggle to rein in his anger. Now that her initial shock had worn off, the whole situation was beginning to take on definite humorous overtones. There was a wicked sparkle in Maggie's blue eyes as she noted Mr. Rafferty's disheveled appearance. His black hair was sticking up in spikes where the woman had obviously run her fingers through it, and there was a bright red lipstick smear all around his mouth. *And* he was bare from the waist up.

Despite her efforts to keep a straight face, Maggie's mouth curled up at the corners when her gaze switched to his companion. She was tall, blond, gorgeous, and busty. Exactly the type adolescent males of all ages fantasized about.

Taking in the scene with a blank, bovine look, the young woman seemed oblivious to the fact that her dress was unbuttoned to her navel, or that her unfettered breasts were in danger of complete exposure.

Hurriedly, Maggie looked away, her eyes darting around in search of a diversion.

To one side of the room the remains of a steak dinner were growing cold on a small candle-lit table set for two. On the hearth there was a plate containing a wedge of ripening Brie and a stem of luscious grapes. Beside it were two barely touched glasses of red wine. Soft, romantic music spilled from stereo speakers hidden somewhere in the corners.

Bubbling laughter began working its way up Maggie's throat, but she swallowed hard and pushed it down. The scene was so obviously set for seduction it was hilarious. *Poor man. No wonder he's so upset. We walked in just as all his careful planning was about to pay off.*

Allison's father cleared his throat noisily. "Yes, well, in that case, I apologize. Why don't you sit down, Mrs. Trent, while the girls go fetch the skates," he said with as much aplomb as possible under the circumstances.

In prudent response to his commanding look, Allison dragged a gaping Laura out into the hall, and a moment later their clamoring footsteps receded up the stairs.

"For God's sake, cover yourself," Clinton Rafferty hissed in an aside to his silent companion as he snatched up his discarded shirt from the floor and shrugged into it.

Maggie's lips twitched when the young woman started guiltily and hastened to comply.

Buttoning his shirt, Clinton Rafferty stalked to the bar in the corner. Maggie bit down hard on her lower lip when she saw him catch sight of his reflection in the mirrored wall behind the bar and hastily snatch up a cocktail napkin to wipe the telltale red smear from around his mouth. She perched on the edge of the sofa, torn between hysterical laughter and acute embarrassment.

"Could I get you a drink, Mrs. Trent?" The question was asked with forced politeness. His stiff face looked as though it would crack at any moment.

"No, thank you."

He returned from the bar with two drinks and handed one to the young woman, who sat down beside Maggie.

"Aren't you gonna introduce me, sugar?" the blonde asked in a wheedling voice, gazing at him seductively.

He winced at the endearment but stretched his

mouth into a parody of a smile and replied smoothly, "Of course. I'm terribly sorry. Bunny, meet Mrs. Trent. Mrs. Trent, this is Bunny Peters."

"Bunny? As in rabbit?" The question popped out before Maggie could stop it, and she was instantly horrified. But to her surprise, the young woman didn't seem in the least offended.

"Yes. Don't you just *love* it? Of course, my real name is Barbara, but I think Bunny suits me better." She glanced at the stony-faced man standing by the fireplace and fluttered her lashes coyly, then looked back at Maggie with a vacuous smile. "You know, 'cause they're always so soft and cuddly."

Maggie stared at her and blinked. Good heavens! The woman's got a forty bustline and an IQ to match, she thought dazedly, swallowing down another giggle.

Looking up, Maggie surprised a chagrined expression on Clinton Rafferty's face and felt a spurt of intense satisfaction. So he's embarrassed by his girlfriend's inane blathering, is he? Good! That's what he gets for romancing juveniles, she told herself gleefully. The girl couldn't have been a day over twenty-one.

Maggie was aware that her host was staring at her dancing eyes and twitching mouth with growing irritation, but she was powerless to do anything about them. The whole situation was so ridiculously funny!

Fortunately, at that moment the girls erupted into the room, and Maggie sighed with relief. She wasn't sure how much longer she could hold her mirth in check.

"I've got my skates, so we're ready to go anytime you are, Mrs. Trent," Allison announced.

Gratefully, Maggie bid good night to Bunny and beat a hasty retreat.

To her dismay, Allison's father walked them all the way to the car and stood patiently by as they buckled themselves in and locked the doors. When she had switched on the ignition, Maggie lowered the window. "Good night, Mr. Rafferty. I'm sorry we intruded." Smiling, she put the car in reverse and started to take her foot off the brake pedal, but then some perverse imp of mischief made her add in a low voice only he could hear, "Oh, by the way. I'd be careful if I were you. Bunnies are said to be terribly prolific, you know."

Not waiting to see his reaction, she stepped on the gas and the car shot down the drive.

Chapter Two

"Gee, Mrs. Trent, I'm sorry about that. I didn't know my dad was going to cook dinner for his date tonight."

"Oh, but you told me—"

Whatever Laura was about to say was cut off by a sharp poke in the ribs from Allison.

Maggie was aware of the bit of byplay but was simply too preoccupied to question it. She was appalled by her own behavior. What on earth had possessed her, making such an awful, outrageous statement? Clinton Rafferty's love life was certainly no business of hers. He was probably livid, and he had every right to be.

"I just wish my dad would date someone nice for a change," Allison sighed wistfully. "His taste in women is the pits."

"Maybe," Laura agreed halfheartedly. "But you've got to admit, his date sure is beautiful."

"Of course she's beautiful. All his girlfriends are beautiful. And they're all so much alike they're practically interchangeable. You know, all gorgeous, young, and dumb.''

The remark was thrown out flippantly, but there was a poignant note of sadness in it that tugged at Maggie's heartstrings.

Hours later, curled up in the corner of the living room sofa, munching popcorn while pretending to watch the late show with the girls, she still could not dismiss Allison's words from her mind. Maggie didn't know who she felt sorrier for—the girl or her father.

Clinton Rafferty was obviously a womanizer, a man incapable of making a deep emotional commitment. It was easy to recognize the breed. She'd been married to one for eleven years.

Maggie sighed, and for the first time in months she allowed herself to think of Larry. Few of her memories were pleasant. Only in the beginning, during their courtship and the early days of their marriage, had she been truly happy. She had been both thrilled and proud when Larry Trent, star quarterback of their college football team and big man on campus, had given her the rush. The single-minded determination with which he pursued her had been especially flattering to a nineteen-year-old, second-year student, and they were married only a week after his graduation. Afterward it hadn't taken Maggie long to realize that for Larry the chase was everything.

How many times in those eleven years had he strayed? And how many times had she forgiven him? It had been a vicious cycle that kept repeating itself over, and over, and over. And still she'd stayed. Not out of love—he had killed whatever feelings she'd had for him years ago—but because to leave, to end it, would have been admitting failure. And failure, to Maggie, never had been and never would be acceptable. It wasn't in her nature to admit defeat.

Her parents, both successful people in their own right, had raised Maggie and her brother, Dennis, to be achievers, instilling in them a deep sense of commitment and pride in a job well done. Whatever Maggie undertook, she gave it her all, whether it was a personal relationship or a business one, and with the exception of her marriage, she had been successful. It had come as a blow to her finally to realize that sometimes your very best simply isn't good enough.

Maggie knew that part of Larry's problem had been an almost fanatical desire to hold on to his youth and relive his days of glory as a football hero. He had been destined for a career in pro ball, but in the final game of his senior year he sustained injuries to his knees that put an end to his football career forever.

But Larry had not been able to adjust. He had grown used to being in the limelight. He needed the adulation of his fans, especially the bevy of beautiful young women that had always surrounded him. For a time he was able to trade on his brief period of fame, but as new heroes appeared people remembered less and less. Frantic, Larry had tried to prove to himself that he still had what it took by becoming involved in a series of affairs. And with each passing year the women got younger and younger.

The end came for Maggie when she returned from a business trip to find him in bed, *their* bed, with a girl still in her teens, and ten-year-old Laura asleep in the next room.

The divorce had become final over two years ago, and though both she and Laura were much happier on their own, the failure of her marriage still ate at her.

The last she'd heard of Larry he had moved to the West Coast and was living life in the fast lane. Maggie no longer loved him, but neither did she hate him. If she felt anything at all it was pity. Men like Larry, and Clinton Rafferty, spent their lives searching for something they were too blind to see.

Maggie's pensive gaze went to the two girls, sprawled inelegantly on the rug in front of the TV. Laura never mentioned her father. But then, Larry hadn't been any better at being a parent than he had at being a husband. Despite Maggie's worries about how the divorce would affect Laura, her daughter seemed quite content with a single parent.

But what about Allison? It was obvious that the child was yearning for something more than her father was providing. Yet it was equally obvious that she adored him, and from the few conversations she'd had with him, Maggie was fairly sure the feeling was mutual.

She was fond of Allison and longed to help in some way, but of course she couldn't, except maybe to provide a sympathetic feminine shoulder to cry on occasionally.

One thing was certain, however, she decided as the TV screen went blank and she and the girls roused themselves to gather up the remains of their snack. She was going to have to apologize to Mr. Rafferty. She'd had absolutely no business shooting off her mouth that way. The girls' continued friendship was more important than scoring points off some arrogant, self-centered male who didn't mean a fig to her anyway.

After her usual jog in the park, Maggie spent the next morning doing housework. With Allison's help, Laura finished her share of the chores in short order. Maggie had just put a load of clothes in the washer and started cleaning the second bathroom when they declared themselves finished and took off for the skating rink.

By shortly after twelve the laundry was done and put

away and the house was sparkling. Maggie was hot, tired, and grubby and longed desperately for a cool shower, but there was one more job left to do.

Maggie snapped on a plastic, coverall-type apron, took shampoo from the cabinet and lifted the large, galvanized washtub from its hook on the utility room wall.

The moment she stepped out onto the patio the enormous Great Dane came loping across the yard, barking an enthusiastic greeting, only to come to a skidding halt a few feet away when he spied the washtub. Ears went back, and the stubby tail ceased its joyous waggle as the huge, fawn-colored head drooped and he looked up at her accusingly from under a piteously furrowed brow. The staccato barking became a mournful whine.

Maggie sat the tub on the brick patio and began to fill it with water from the garden hose. She gave the recalcitrant dog a stern look. "Now you can just cut that out, Tiny, because it's not going to do you one bit of good. It's time for your bath, so just get over here," she commanded in a no-nonsense tone, pointing an imperious finger toward the rapidly filling tub.

The rebuke halted the woeful complaint, and Tiny slunk forward in abject canine misery. If he'd had more than a nub for a tail, it would have been between his legs.

"Oh, you're just a big baby," Maggie scolded as the dog stepped into the water with jerky reluctance.

For the next half-hour Tiny stood semi-docilely while Maggie lathered and scrubbed, the muscles under the fawn coat quivering with distaste, his black-muzzled face the picture of dejection.

It was a difficult job for Maggie, as the dog was a giant even among his own breed. When she was barefoot Tiny had only to lift his head to lick the tip of her chin, and he outweighed her by a good seventy pounds. But for all his great size, Tiny was a lamb, at least as far as Maggie and Laura were concerned. His absolute devotion to them made him putty in their hands, but Maggie was fairly certain that if anyone attempted to harm them he would probably take their leg off.

When at last the dog was clean and rinsed, Maggie gave the command for him to step out, then ducked for cover, laughing as Tiny tried to shake himself dry, sending showers of water out fifteen feet in every direction. When he had finished, she patted him with an old towel and then led him into the utility room.

"Down, Tiny," she ordered, pointing to the rug where he was to stay until he was thoroughly dry. Familiar with the routine and happy to have his weekly ordeal over, Tiny obeyed with alacrity.

Maggie had just closed the utility room door and started for the stairs when the doorbell rang.

"Oh, good grief! What now?" Determined to get rid of whoever it was in short order, she stalked toward the front door, her bare feet making small slapping sounds on the parquet floor.

Without thinking, she jerked the door open and immediately sucked in a startled breath. Unconsciously the fingers gripping the edge of the door tightened, making the knuckles white. She had to fight the urge to slam the door shut again and pretend he wasn't there.

Gone was the disheveled man of the night before. Today Clinton Rafferty's thick black hair was brushed and smooth, and his face was newly shaved. He wore a green cotton shirt and a pair of faded, well-worn jeans that fit his long muscular thighs like a second skin and did absolutely nothing to disguise his masculinity. The top three buttons of the casual shirt were open, revealing a thatch of dark hair covering a broad, bronzed chest.

Tearing her gaze away from the tantalizing view, Maggie looked up and met his eyes. They were emerald. Glittering. Mesmerizing.

Maggie's heart began to pound. She was suddenly painfully aware of her bare feet and tacky cutoffs and T-shirt. Self-consciously, she tried to brush a wisp of hair away from her face.

Why? Why did he have to show up when I look like an unmade bed?

Oh darn! What difference does it make, she derided herself sternly.

Taking a deep breath, she forced what she hoped was a pleasant smile to her face. "Good afternoon, Mr. Rafferty. Won't you come in?"

"Hello, Mrs. Trent." Once inside he turned and handed her a brown paper sack. He seemed strangely ill at ease. "Allison forgot her allergy medicine. I thought she might need it."

"Oh, I see. Well, I . . . uh . . . I'll be sure and give it to her." When he didn't respond Maggie added hesitantly, "I . . . uh . . . I'm afraid the girls aren't here right now. They've gone to the skating rink."

"I see."

Despite his laconic reply Maggie was encouraged. She had expected him to be angry, but evidently he wasn't. Both his voice and expression were politely neutral. Gathering her courage, she drew herself up to her full five feet two inches. "Mr. Rafferty, about last night," she began diffidently, "I want to apologize for my remark. I had no business saying what I did. I'm afraid I have a rather cockeyed sense of humor, and sometimes it gets the best of me."

He eyed her intently, then allowed his mouth to quirk upward at the corners. "Apology accepted."

Maggie sighed with relief. "Thank you."

"I think, for the sake of the girls, we should wipe the slate clean and start over." Clint smiled and raised his brows questioningly. "Don't you?"

"Yes, I'm sure that would be best."

Eyes twinkling, he stuck out his hand and said gravely, "How do you do, Mrs. Trent. I'm Clinton Rafferty."

After the merest hesitation, Maggie grinned and accepted the handshake, feeling a tingling sensation race up her arm as her soft palm came into contact with his warm, calloused one.

Silently chiding herself for the foolish response, she pulled her hand free. She glanced up at him nervously and smiled. "Look, I was about to get cleaned up, then have lunch. If you wouldn't mind waiting in the living room for a few minutes, I'd be happy to have you join me."

"I have a better idea. Why don't you show me the kitchen and let me get started on lunch while you shower?" His teasing smile was wide and white and made Maggie's insides quiver strangely. "I open a mean can of soup."

"Oh, I don't know . . ."

"I promise you I know my way around a kitchen. Allison and I have been on our own for five years now. It was either learn to cook or starve."

Maggie bit her lip and looked at him uncertainly. She was torn between her duty as a hostess and the desire to shed the grubby clothes and stand under a refreshing shower. The shower finally won. She told herself she simply wanted to be clean and presentable. She certainly wasn't trying to appear attractive for Clinton

Rafferty. "Well, if you're sure . . ." She let the sentence trail into silence and turned to lead the way down the central hall to the kitchen at the back of the house.

"Very nice," he said, taking in the cheery, functional room. Blue and white checkered wallpaper covered two thirds of the walls above white painted wainscoting. The counter tops were stark white, man-made marble, and the backsplash was covered with hand-painted blue and white delft tiles. The cabinets were a rich pecan wood. A wicker basket hanging above the sink contained an English ivy whose graceful, trailing arms spilled over the edge and cascaded downward like a delicate green waterfall.

"Thanks," she replied, pulling a can of tomato soup from the cupboard and placing it on the counter. "The pots are in the bottom cabinet next to the dishwasher, and there are sandwich makings in the refrigerator, along with soft drinks, if you like."

Maggie took off her apron and stood for a moment in the middle of the floor, undecided about what to do with it. She could hear Tiny's pleading whine from inside the utility room. She knew if she returned it to its proper place the dog would come bounding out to investigate their visitor. With a shrug, she went to the pantry and hung it on the inside of the door.

"Oh!"

The word came out in a startled gasp when Maggie turned to find Clinton Rafferty standing only a few inches away.

He grinned wickedly and leaned forward, bracing his arms on either side of her. Swallowing hard, her eyes growing round, Maggie flattened herself against the door. His devilish green eyes raked over her petite body, all the way from her slightly askew topknot to her bare feet, lingering along the way on her breasts and the womanly roundness of her hips.

"You're a little bitty thing, aren't you," he observed in a husky voice that wasn't much more than a whisper.

Maggie's mouth dropped open in astonishment, then a blue flame leaped in her eyes. "Now just a darned minute. . . ."

"But I will say, you're curved in all the right places and perfectly proportioned," he continued as though unaware of her growing ire. "And you've got great legs. In that getup you look like a pint-sized pinup. How in the world is a man supposed to resist?"

Maggie fully intended to tell him, but before she could form the scathing retort his mouth swooped to cover hers in a burning kiss that made her toes curl against the cool tile floor.

He wasted no time claiming the territory her parted lips had left open to his invasion. His tongue quickly delved into the sweetness of her mouth, stroking, probing, rubbing against hers with bold familiarity.

He was only touching her with his lips, yet their warm, insistent pressure held her pinned against the door. She could feel the hard, flat surface pressing against the back of her head and all along the length of her spine.

Maggie's heart was knocking against her ribs. Her hands flattened against the door, her spread fingers gripping desperately for a hold. She was so stunned she couldn't have moved if her very life depended on it.

But if her reasoning power was blunted, her sensory perception was acute. She was sharply aware of the musky male scent of him, mingled with a hint of soap and a spicy masculine cologne, of the taste of him in her mouth, the heat that radiated from his body. She felt the warm firmness of his lips slanted across hers. She even heard the thunder of his heart—or was it hers?—in the quiet of the room. She felt on fire all the way to the soles of her feet.

The kiss seemed to go on and on forever, as though time had ceased to exist. But finally, just when Maggie thought her knees would buckle, he drew away and smiled down at her with lazy, male satisfaction.

Maggie stared back, unable to speak or move, her eyes unblinking. She dragged several long gulps of air into her lungs and struggled for a toehold on reality. As her breathing began to slow to normal her mind cleared, and with the clearing came rationality. Following close on its heels was anger.

"What the devil do you think you're doing?" she demanded in a strangled voice, glaring up at him with flaming blue eyes.

Clint gave her a look of wounded innocence. "Why, I'm just following directions." Then he grinned mischievously, his green eyes twinkling as he pointed to her shirt.

Bewildered, Maggie looked down and gasped. She had fallen into the habit of using Laura's old, discarded T-shirts for jogging and working around the house during the warm months. This morning she had pulled a clean one from the drawer and slipped it on without giving it a thought. Laura, like many teenagers, had a penchant for wearing shirts that sported outrageous, sometimes shocking slogans and messages. Maggie had grown so accustomed to them she hardly gave them a thought. Now she flushed guiltily as she realized that emblazoned across her breasts in bold script were the words "Kiss me, you fool!"

Battling her embarrassment, she eyed him accusingly and snapped, "You didn't have to take it literally!"

"Oh, it was my pleasure," he assured her with a mock seriousness that made her want to slap him.

"Now listen to me, Mr. Rafferty! When I agreed to start over, I meant as friends, as fellow parents, nothing more. Is that clear? *Whatever* gave you the idea you could come waltzing in here and treat me like one of your little"—a grimace of distaste twisted Maggie's mouth as she groped for a suitable description—"little Playboy bunnies!" she spat out finally.

"Feisty little thing, aren't you," he said, grinning.

"*Mr. Rafferty.*" His name was ground out through clenched teeth, a warning implicit in the low, furious tone.

"Okay, okay. If that's the way you want it," he said, chuckling. Pushing himself away from the door, he straightened up to his full height and rubbed the back of his neck, rotating his head from side to side. "It's probably just as well. I've got a crick in my neck from bending over so far."

A reluctant smile pulled at the corners of Maggie's mouth. "Serves you right," she muttered, not quite hiding the hint of laughter behind her words. "I think you'd better stick to tall, stacked blondes."

"Maybe you're right." Clint acknowledged the little dig with a wry, self-mocking twist of his mouth.

He picked up the can of soup from the counter and rummaged through a drawer until he found an opener. "Now why don't you scoot on upstairs and have that shower while I get started on our lunch," he tossed over his shoulder. "I don't know about you, but I'm starving."

Maggie stared, torn between lingering anger and astonishment. Just like that, he was going to dismiss the whole episode? One minute he's coming on to her with all the subtlety of a sailor on a three-hour pass, and the next he's calmly preparing lunch? She didn't know whether to be relieved or furious. At a loss, she watched him search the cabinets for a pot, then finally, with an ironic lift of her hands, she turned on her heel and walked out. "He certainly knows how to make himself at home," she groused under her breath as the sounds of clanging utensils and masculine humming followed her up the stairs.

Spurred on by the knowledge that there was a strange male loose in her kitchen, Maggie showered and washed her hair in record time. After dressing in a pair of cinnamon slacks and a cinnamon and white striped cotton knit pullover with three-quarter sleeves, she applied a light coating of makeup and then started on her hair.

As she wielded the blow dryer and brush, shaping the rich brown mane into its customary glossy bell, her face wore a pensive look.

Why, she wondered, was she always attracted to rogues? For that was exactly what Clinton Rafferty was: a charming, devilishly handsome rogue. And she was *definitely* attracted. Not even to herself could she deny that. The moment she laid eyes on him she had been aware of the pull of his sensual magnetism, had felt that exciting tingle that occurs when the chemistry is right between a man and woman.

Maggie sighed and yanked the brush through her hair with a vengeance. She didn't want to feel that way about Allison's father. It would only bring her heartache, and *that* she didn't need. She'd had eleven years' worth of it from Larry.

Though the way things looked, she probably didn't have anything to worry about on that score. Mr. Rafferty had certainly given in easily on the matter of their future relationship. She had been prepared to do battle, expecting him to brush aside her protest. As much as she hated to admit it, his failure to do so had rankled.

Maggie switched off the dryer and gave her hair one last flick with the brush. Leaning close to the mirror, she scowled. "Perverse creature," she muttered at her reflection.

Slowly, the scowl became an impudent grin. She might be attracted to that good-looking scoundrel, but she wasn't about to become involved with him. Only a fool would make the same mistake twice. Besides, even if it was what she wanted, she could never be part of his interchangeable set of girlfriends. She wasn't gorgeous *or* young. And she certainly wasn't dumb.

Chuckling to herself, Maggie padded to the closet and surveyed the numerous shoes lined up neatly on the rack along one wall. They were all high-heeled except for two pairs, and those were her scruffy jogging shoes and a pair of fuzzy house slippers.

Maggie glanced wistfully at her pink toes, sunk deep into the thick pile of the carpet, and with a resigned sigh stepped into a pair of high-heeled sandals. One of the disadvantages of being only five foot two, Maggie reflected disgustedly, was you spent half your time tottering around on ridiculously high heels in an effort to look taller, only to spend the other half running around barefoot because your feet hurt so damned much. Her propensity for shedding her shoes at every opportunity earned her a lot of good-natured kidding from her fellow workers at Channel 6, but Maggie didn't care. In her own office, at home, and anywhere else it was possible, she went unshod.

But today she needed the extra boost that high heels gave her, not only in height, but in confidence.

When she entered the kitchen Clint was just ladling the steaming tomato soup into two bowls. The table in the breakfast nook was set with green quilted place mats, white ironstone, and her deep blue handblown tumblers. In the center sat a platter heaped with ham and cheese sandwiches.

"My, you *have* been busy," Maggie commented in faint surprise.

He looked up from his chore and grinned. His

encompassing glance quickly took in the changes in her appearance, from her shining hair all the way down. The grin grew wider when he reached the spiked heels. "Soup and sandwiches are a snap," he said breezily. "Sometime you'll have to taste what I can do with a sirloin steak."

Maggie let the remark slide with a noncommital smile. If last night were any example, his steak dinners were a bit too spicy for her taste. She crossed to the refrigerator and opened the door. "What would you like to drink? Iced tea, soft drink, or milk?"

"Tea will be fine." He placed the soup on the table while Maggie filled the glasses, then held her chair politely.

Neither spoke for several minutes. To Maggie's disgust, she found his nearness unsettling. She felt strangely tense, like an overwound spring, and hadn't the slightest idea what to do about it.

Slowly, methodically, she spooned the soup into her mouth and watched him through the downward sweep of her lashes.

If only he weren't so damned good to look at.

He took a sandwich, sank his teeth into it, and chewed with relish. A painful tightness attacked Maggie's throat as she watched the up and down movements of his strong jaw, the rhythmic flex of muscles in his lean cheeks.

Maggie tried another spoonful of soup and discovered that it suddenly hurt to swallow.

How perfectly stupid! she berated herself scathingly. He's only a man. Strong, attractive, and virile, but essentially no different from any other. Slanting him a defiant look, she bit off a healthy chunk of sandwich, chewed furiously, and washed it down with a swig of iced tea.

"What do you do for a living, Mr. Rafferty?" Maggie

asked, determinedly squelching the unsettling reactions. "I don't believe Allison has ever said."

He laid his spoon down on his plate and smiled at her. "Don't you think we could dispense with the formality now? My name is Clinton. Most people call me Clint."

Unaccountably tongue-tied under his intent stare, Maggie took a quick sip of tea and cleared her throat. "Mine's Maggie." Her mouth twisted into a wry grimace. "Well, actually it's Margaret, but I've been called Maggie ever since I can remember."

"Maggie?" He looked up sharply, his expression first surprised, then thoughtful. There was a hint of a frown between his thick, black brows. He picked up his spoon again and stirred his soup slowly, watching the steam rise in curling wisps. "I believe Allison said something about you being in television. What is it you do, exactly?"

"I'm the producer of 'Houston Today.' That's an afternoon talk show," she added in case he wasn't yet familiar with the local programs.

To Maggie's amazement his expression became even more somber. She picked up a pepper mill and ground a few flakes into her soup, watching him thoughtfully. Did he have something against television?

"You still haven't told me what business you're in," she reminded him.

He looked up and smiled, seeming to shake off his dark preoccupation. "I guess you could say I'm in retail sales."

His eyes twinkled at her mysteriously, and for a second Maggie forgot to breathe. The question of his employment was no longer important. That wide, white smile was devastating. And his eyes . . . they were such a vivid, clear green. Like emeralds.

She pulled herself up short and took another bite of her sandwich, chewing forcefully, as though she were grinding up rocks. *Easy girl, easy. The man may be charming and sexy as hell, but he's still a rogue. And you'd be wise not to forget it.*

By applying herself assiduously to her food and limiting herself to only quick glances in his direction, Maggie managed to get through the rest of the meal with her composure still intact.

When they finished, Clint helped her to clear the table, then stood leaning against the counter with his arms crossed over his chest, watching as she loaded the dishwasher. Maggie determinedly kept the conversation centered on the girls and their blossoming friendship. It was a safe topic. Clint was obviously a loving father and deeply concerned about his daughter's happiness. He seemed as pleased as she about the bond between the girls.

When the kitchen was clean, Maggie dried her hands on a towel and stood uncertainly. An awkward silence stretched between them. She deliberately did not ask him to stay. He was too potent, too dangerous to her peace of mind.

After a brief hesitation, Clint pushed himself away from the counter. "Well, I guess I'd better be going. Thanks for the lunch."

"Thank *you* for preparing it," Maggie said sincerely.

"Listen, since the girls are practically inseparable, how about letting Laura spend next weekend at our place?" he asked pleasantly when they paused in the foyer.

Maggie twisted her hands together worriedly. This was something she hadn't counted on. Her mind groped for a plausible excuse to deny his request, but none came. Finally she realized she had no choice but to tell him the truth and hope he would understand.

"No, I . . . uh . . . really don't think that would be a good idea."

"Why not?"

"Look, Clint," Maggie began in a reasoning tone. "You're a single man, and I suppose it's only natural that you would have a rather free and easy life style, but . . . well . . . to tell you the truth, I would prefer that Laura not be exposed to the kind of scene we stumbled onto last night. So I think it would be best all around if—"

"Why you little prig!"

The harsh denunciation cut off Maggie's words as effectively as a slap. She bit her lower lip and watched apprehensively as his face tightened with rage. His eyes narrowed into two glittering green slits.

"I admit to having the normal, healthy male's appetite for sex, but credit me with a little discretion, at least. For your information, Miss Prude, I never bring my female companions to the house when Allison is at home. But even so, these days most thirteen year olds are well aware of the facts of life."

His caustic words sent Maggie's own temper soaring. Her petite body grew rigid, and her chin thrust out belligerently. "Awareness is one thing. A live demonstration is something else!" she snapped. "And regardless of what you say, it was fairly obvious last night that Allison wasn't exactly shocked to find you in a clinch with that young girl!"

"Is that what's bugging you? The fact that she was young?"

"Why should it bother me?" Maggie gave him a saccharine-sweet smile and blinked innocently. "Actually, it's probably very wise of you to date young girls. Just think, if you marry your Bunny Rabbit you'll be getting not only a bed partner but a playmate for Allison as well," she purred.

He stared at her for several tense seconds, his nostrils quivering with suppressed fury. Then, leaning forward from the waist, he brought his face down to within inches of hers and snarled, "You've got a mean tongue on you, lady. You know that?"

"Why, whatever is the matter, Mr. Rafferty?" she asked guilelessly. "Does the truth hurt?"

"Why you little—"

There was a sudden cry of alarm from the back of the house, followed by a hair-raising animal yowl that sent Tiny into a paroxysm of barking.

Startled, both Maggie and Clint swung toward the sound, wearing identical astonished expressions.

"Catch him, quick!" Laura hollered.

Something hit the utility room door with a thud, sending it flying open, and in the next instant a ball of gray-blue fur came streaking across the kitchen toward the door leading into the hall. Beyond, the scene in the utility was pure bedlam.

Laura and Allison were scrambling around the tiny room in a tangle of arms and legs, bumping into walls, appliances, and each other in a desperate attempt to subdue the frenzied dog. Somehow they both managed to grab hold of his collar, but even their combined strength couldn't hold him.

"Heel, Tiny! Heel!" Laura yelled.

Tiny's paws scrabbled on the tile floor, and with a mighty lunge he broke Allison's hold, sending her staggering backward to fall flat on her backside. "Hold him! Hold him! Don't let him get away!" she screeched.

Laura dug in her heels and hung on for a few seconds, but she was no match for the hundred-and-seventy-pound bundle of fury. Two steps inside the kitchen he broke free and turned on the speed.

The blue fur ball tore down the central hallway,

headed straight as an arrow for Maggie and Clint. Directly behind him, in hot pursuit, came Tiny.

The girls were yelling, "Stop him! Stop him!" Tiny's sharp, deep-throated barks were running together, bouncing off the walls of the hallway like rolling thunder, and his quarry, which Maggie recognized as their neighbor's cat, Wilfred, was yowling like a banshee. A tornado ripping through the house couldn't have created more noise and confusion.

Wilfred took dead aim at Clint and zipped between his legs into the living room.

With single-minded determination, Tiny attempted to do the same. He hit the man at full speed and tried to plow his way through the obstacle of iron-muscled thighs.

"What the hell!" Clint shouted as his legs were knocked out from under him and he toppled forward onto Tiny's back.

Man and dog went down together, but before Clint could recover Tiny was scrambling out from under him to resume the chase. He made the turn into the living room at nearly top speed, skidding on the polished parquet floor and slamming into the wall before regaining his footing.

The girls came running into the hall and stopped dead still at the sight of Allison's father sprawled face down on the floor, trying to recover his breath. Eyes round, mouths slack, they slowly turned their heads and gaped at one another in absolute horror.

"Sweet, jumping Jehoshaphat," Allison croaked in a barely audible whisper.

Maggie's astonished stare went from the downed man to the horror-stricken girls, and back. Then, as though in slow motion, she sagged against the wall and gave in to a fit of helpless laughter.

In the living room Wilfred clawed his way up over the

top of a high-backed Queen Anne chair, then cleared the coffee table in one leap and bounced to the sofa. With the tracking tenacity of a Pathfinder missile, Tiny followed suit. Anything that got in their way was knocked over.

Clint had just managed to restart his lungs and struggle to his hands and knees when the pair shot out the door again.

Wilfred clawed for purchase over Clint's back and shoulders, eliciting a yelp of pain from the abused man and more cries of alarm from the girls. Tiny's front paws hit him squarely between the shoulder blades before the sounds had died away, and Clint went down like a pole-axed steer, sliding forward across the waxed floor, arms and legs flailing.

Maggie's knees gave way beneath her, and she slid down the wall and collapsed on the floor, clutching her sides as tears streamed down her face.

The three-tiered plant stand beside the newel post toppled as Clint slammed into the stairs, hitting the floor with a resounding crash and sending shards of ceramic pots, dirt, and mangled African violets in all directions. At about the same time the animals left the house via the open back door. Suddenly the quiet was deafening.

"Daddy! Daddy, are you all right?"

Allison's frightened voice brought Maggie back to her senses, and she swallowed down the hysterical laughter that bubbled up in her throat. Holding her sides, she climbed to her feet and picked her way gingerly through the debris, reaching Clint's side just as the girls helped him into a sitting position.

One look at the blood streaming down his face and Maggie sobered. "Laura, go wet some towels in cold water and bring them here," she ordered. "Quickly!"

While the terrified girl sped away, Maggie conducted

a quick search for other injuries, sighing with relief when none were found.

When Laura returned, Maggie pressed a wet cloth to Clint's forehead to staunch the flow of blood. Using another, she attempted to mop up his face.

"I'm terribly sorry about this, Clint. Tiny is usually very well behaved. It's just that he goes berserk whenever he sees our neighbor's cat. And the wretched creature seems to know it. Sometimes I think he deliberately torments the dog."

"Dog? *Dog?* You call that animal a *dog?*" Clint demanded indignantly, snatching the cloth from her and pressing it to the wound himself. He glowered at her darkly. "That's not a *dog,* lady, that's a small horse!" Waving away their attempts to help, he struggled to his feet. Wordlessly, he accepted the clean towel she handed him in exchange for the blood-soaked one and stared down at her through squinted eyes. "Tiny?" he said incredulously, as though the name had only just registered. "You call that . . . that . . . *behemoth* Tiny?"

His outraged expression was almost too much for Maggie. She could feel the laughter threatening to break loose again. Lips twitching, she gave him a guileless look and shrugged. "Well, he *was* tiny when we got him. The cutest little ball of fur you ever saw."

"God give me strength," Clint groaned.

"Daddy, shouldn't you go to the hospital and have someone look at that cut?" Allison interjected, nervously plucking at his sleeve.

"She's right," Maggie agreed. "I'm sure it needs some stitches. Come on. I'll drive you. There's a hospital just a few miles from here." She stepped forward to take his arm, but he wouldn't allow it.

"No, thanks. I'm perfectly capable of driving myself."

"Oh, but—"

"Mrs. Trent! It isn't safe for me to be in the same room with you, much less in a car."

"But that's silly," she protested.

"Is it? Then suppose you tell me why it is," he asked with exaggerated patience, pronouncing every word slowly and precisely, "that every time I get around you disaster strikes?"

For a full ten seconds Maggie stared at him in astonishment. Then, slowly, her brows rose and she spread her hands wide, palms up.

"Can I help it if you're accident prone?"

Chapter Three

The door was slammed so hard it rattled the glass in the side panels flanking it. Head held high, Maggie stared at the closed portal with a ghost of a smile hovering around her mouth.

Her sense of victory turned to dust, however, when she turned and encountered the girls' stricken faces. They couldn't have looked more disheartened if television had suddenly been outlawed.

"Hey, you two. There's no reason to look so sad," Maggie chided teasingly. "It isn't the end of the world, you know." Her warm gaze held compassion and just a hint of apology when she looked at Allison. "I know you're disappointed that your dad and I can't seem to get along, but that's the way things go sometimes. Don't worry, though. Just because we rub each other the wrong way doesn't mean that you and Laura can't be friends."

"What was my dad doing here, anyway?" Allison asked forlornly.

"He came by to bring your allergy medicine, and since I was about to have lunch I invited him to stay."

Adopting a brisk air, Maggie turned away from the two dejected faces and surveyed Tiny and Wilfred's path of destruction. The hall was littered with dirt and broken pottery and pathetic pieces of wilted plant life. The top tier of the mahogany plant stand had broken in two, and the Oriental rug at the base of the stairs was crumpled up like a wet dishrag and spotted with Clint Rafferty's blood.

In the living room two lamps lay drunkenly on the carpet, their shades dented and askew. The overturned magazine rack had spilled its contents on the rug like a fanned out deck of giant playing cards, and there wasn't a single ornament or ashtray left on any of the tables. The pile of needlepoint throw pillows that usually resided on the sofa was scattered to the four corners of the room. One, curiously, had landed on top of the tall secretary desk in the corner.

Maggie sighed. "Okay, girls, why don't you go get the broom and dustpan and clean up this mess while I see what I can do in here," she instructed, stepping through the door into the living room.

"Do you *believe* this?" Laura moaned as soon as they were out of her mother's hearing. "After that little episode, we'll be lucky if they ever speak to each other again! We've got about as much chance of getting them married now as we have of spitting on the moon. I mean, let's face it, Allison. We bombed out."

"I thought so at first, too," Allison said excitedly. "But I was wrong. Things are going to work out just fine."

Laura jerked to a halt and stared at her friend as though she had lost her mind. "Are you nuts? How can you say that after that . . . that . . . Keystone Cops routine we just went through? You're dad was as mad as a hornet when he stomped out of here. And my mom is none too pleased with him either, I can tell you. So how do you figure things are just fine?"

"Because, silly, Dad brought my allergy medicine over."

"So?"

"So, I only get allergies in the spring, and this is the end of September," Allison explained with smug superiority. "Dad just used that as an excuse to come over, which means he's definitely interested. All we have to do now is see to it that he stays interested." She frowned and pursed her lips. "Of course, it would have been better if your mom hadn't laughed at him. Men have such fragile egos, you know. But then, on second thought, that may not have been so bad. Women usually fall all over themselves trying to please Dad. No one has ever laughed at him before," she said in a thoughtful tone, then added softly, "except maybe my mom."

"And just exactly how are we supposed to keep him interested?" Laura demanded, still not convinced.

Allison lifted the broom from its hook on the utility room wall and started back toward the foyer. "I don't know yet, but don't worry, I'll think of something."

An hour later, when he stalked into his study, Clint's face was set in grim lines. Tossing the packet of pain pills the doctor had given him onto his desk, he went to the liquor cabinet and poured out a stiff measure of whiskey. He took a long swallow and filled his glass again, then sat down in the leather chair behind the desk and stared broodingly at nothing, absently fingering the bandage above his left brow.

"You really made an ass of yourself this time,

Rafferty," he muttered angrily. *Why in hell had he gone over there in the first place?* Maggie Trent was not the type of woman to fit into the life he had made for himself. That had been obvious last night.

As she had sat beside Bunny on the sofa the comparison between the two women had been almost cruel. Maggie's delicate, wholesome beauty and vibrant personality, to say nothing of her outrageous sense of humor, had made the younger girl seem tawdry, dull, and incredibly stupid.

He had been angry with her for making him so sharply aware of his date's shortcomings and for being amused by the awkward situation. He had been glad to see her go, sure that he and Bunny could pick up where they had left off. Clint snorted disgustedly. What a joke! Try as he might, he had been unable to shake off his dissatisfaction. He lifted the whiskey glass to his mouth. He swallowed the fiery liquid and chuckled mirthlessly. Bunny had been mad as hell when he hustled her out only a few minutes after the others had left.

Sobering, Clint put the glass down on his desk. The tumbler's thick bottom hit the wood with a loud thud. He had been foolish to go over there. The attraction he felt for Laura's mother could never come to anything. Maggie Trent was not the kind for a casual affair or a one-night stand, and that was all he could offer any woman.

No, Maggie was the kind you took home to meet your folks, the kind you built dreams around, planned a future with.

Clint's somber gaze went to the gold-framed picture on the corner of the desk. Reaching out with one long finger, he touched the woman's smiling face and sighed. He had done all that once. For ten years he and Elaine had loved and fought and supported one another through good times and bad, sharing a life that had given him utter happiness and contentment. But with her death that life had ended. He didn't believe it was possible to find that kind of perfect love more than once. And he'd had his.

To Maggie's relief the rest of the weekend passed without incident. That evening she and the girls went to a pizza parlor for dinner and then took in a movie. On Sunday morning they attended church, and after a huge midday meal, Laura and Allison spent the rest of the day upstairs in Laura's room, talking and giggling conspiratorially, while Maggie curled up on the sofa with a new historical novel she'd been wanting to read.

By the time she arrived at the station on Monday morning she had all but put Saturday's fiasco and Clinton Rafferty out of her mind. When Alex popped into her office to ask how the weekend went she even managed to smile and say "Fine" without cringing.

As they had arranged, Selene Bentley came by the station at noon to pick up Maggie and Alex for their luncheon with Henry Burk and his mystery partner. Selene, a tall, stylish woman in her mid-fifties, was the executive who handled the Sporting Chance account for Milford and Stone Advertising Agency. Cool, aggressive, and sharp as a tack, she was the epitome of the modern career woman, but she was also an old and dear friend of Mary and Tim Sullivan, Maggie's parents. It had been on Selene's recommendation that Maggie had been hired at KRHX-TV ten years ago. Selene was mentor, friend, and honorary aunt all rolled into one. Maggie knew that as long as Selene felt it was in her client's best interest, she would support Maggie's efforts to keep Henry Burk as the show's major sponsor.

Though Selene knew the identity of Henry's new

partner, she steadfastly refused to reveal it. "You'll find out soon enough," she replied tauntingly to Maggie's persistent probing, as she threaded her sleek Cadillac through the snarl of Houston's midday traffic. "Besides, I think Henry wants to surprise you. Even though he's been retired a few years, the man is something of a legend in the sports world, and Henry is tickled pink over the partnership."

"If *I* recognize him it *will* be a surprise," was Maggie's disgruntled reply, which drew a smile of understanding from Selene. Life with Larry had given her an aversion to professional sports, and for the last ten years she had avoided them like the plague. The only sports figure she would even recognize, either by name or sight, was Joe Namath, and that was only because of his pantyhose commercials.

Maggie stared out the side window and absently fingered the ruffle at her wrist. The rose and pink silk dress had long full sleeves and a softly draped collar that drew attention to the graceful arch of her neck. It was easily the most feminine dress she owned, which was exactly why she had chosen to wear it today. It was her experience that most jocks preferred to think of women as fragile, defenseless creatures. While she had no desire to attract Henry's new partner, Maggie certainly wasn't against using whatever psychological advantage was available.

Henry and his partner were already seated when they arrived at the restaurant. After they identified themselves, they were quickly escorted across the elegant dining room to a corner table where the two men were waiting. Sandwiched in line between Selene and Alex, Maggie didn't get a clear view of either of them until they came to a halt beside the table.

"Selene! Maggie! It's good to see you," Henry greeted genially as he and his companion rose to their feet. "You too, of course, Alex," he added with a laugh, thumping the younger man's shoulder.

Vaguely, Maggie felt her hand being engulfed in their sponsor's beefy one. "I . . . uh . . . it's nice to see you too, Henry," she managed to stammer, but her eyes were glued to the tall, dark man at his side.

"Hello, Maggie." Clinton Rafferty's smile was sly and knowing, mocking. Swallowing hard, Maggie stared at him in complete shock, unable to utter a sound.

When Henry released it, Clint took her limp hand between both of his and held her gaze with a warm, intimate look. "It's nice to see you again," he murmured in a husky tone that sent a strange tingle sliding down her spine. The smile grew slowly wider, and his green eyes danced with devilish enjoyment as they roamed over Maggie's stunned face.

His obvious amusement finally snapped Maggie out of her stupor, and with a haughty lift of her chin she pulled her hand free. "Hello, Mr. Rafferty," she said in a cool, distant voice. Slowly, deliberately, she let her eyes settle on the bandage above his left eye, and she smiled. "How's the head?"

"Three stitches and a little soreness," he answered with a lopsided grin. "I think I'll live."

Damn the man! He had known all along! And he hadn't said a word! Maggie railed silently, keeping a stiff smile pasted to her face. Frantically, she struggled to recall everything she'd said to him, then winced when she did. Oh God, why did *he* have to be Henry's new partner?

Her eyes narrowed as she contemplated his smug expression. He had known who she was from the moment she told him about her job, which accounted for those strange looks she'd received at lunch Saturday. Yet he had blithely told her he was in retail sales.

Some retail sales! That was like saying the Grand Canyon was a hole in the ground. True, but hardly descriptive.

"Maggie, you sly devil. You didn't tell me you knew Clint Rafferty," Alex chided eagerly.

"Maggie and I met only recently," Clint explained, giving Alex's hand a firm shake. "But we do have a lot in common."

"Wait a minute! Rafferty. Rafferty." Alex's stunned gaze went from Maggie to Clint, then back. "You don't mean to tell me this is Allison's father?" he asked incredulously.

"I see my daughter's fame has preceded me," Clint said, laughing. He smiled at Henry and Selene's bemused expressions and added, "The fact is that in the month since we moved here my daughter and Maggie's have become best friends. And that being the case, Maggie and I . . . ah—"grinning crookedly, he paused and gave Maggie a devilish look, once again fingering the bandage above his eyes—"spent a few hours this past weekend getting to know one another."

Selene arched a brow at this piece of news. "How nice that you two are already on friendly terms," she drawled, lowering her elegantly bony frame into one of the plush chairs surrounding the table. "It does make business negotiations so much easier."

Maggie barely stifled a groan. *Easier, ha! If Selene only knew!*

It wasn't until everyone was seated that Maggie realized she had somehow been maneuvered between Henry and Clint. Slowly it began to sink in that she was the only one at the table who hadn't the foggiest idea exactly *who* Clint Rafferty was, and she squirmed uncomfortably. From the way Alex was almost fawning over him, Maggie could only assume he was, indeed, a celebrity among sports fans, but nothing she'd heard so far had given her a clue as to why.

At that moment, to Maggie's great relief, a waiter appeared. While the others made small talk, Maggie remained quiet and studied her menu with intense concentration. Even so, she was vitally aware of the man at her side. From the corner of her eye she caught every movement of those large, capable hands, each subtle shift of his leanly muscled body. Helplessly, her heart thumping in her tight chest, Maggie noted the sharp contrast between the white cuff and his darkly tanned skin, the crisp dark hairs scattered over the back of his hands, the blunt, well-cared-for nails.

When the waiter returned a few minutes later, Maggie jerked her eyes back to her menu and promptly ordered a gargantuan meal. Healthy in the best of times, her appetite reached alarming proportions when she was under stress. She could not help but notice the way Clint's brows rose as she reeled off her choices, but she ignored him and under cover of the table slipped her feet from the tortuous four-inch sling pumps. A full stomach and bare feet were the best tension reducers she knew of.

"Well, now, since we all know why we're here, I suggest we get right to it," Henry said when the waiter retreated toward the kitchen. He fixed Maggie with a direct stare that held a wealth of apology. "My dear, you know that I'm pleased with the job you people at Channel 6 have done and that I think the *Houston Today* show is a high-quality program, but . . . well, the truth is, Clint here has a few objections to sponsoring the show, and after listening to his reasons, I've got to admit they make sense."

Turning her head, Maggie met Clint's steady green gaze and arched her brow. "And just what are your reasons, Mr. Rafferty?" Besides wanting to get even, she added silently.

The fractional hardening of his face told her he had read the silent accusation in her eyes, but his voice was steady and sure, totally controlled. "First of all, the show is on too early in the day to reach the majority of our customers, most of whom are at work at that hour. Secondly, I think the tone of the show is too highbrow to attract the audience we're aiming for. Last week you had as guests an economist who had written a book on investments, a psychologist, a concert pianist, and a Shakespearean actor. None of those people or the topics they discussed would hold any great appeal for a sportsman."

"Really?" Maggie questioned archly. "Please forgive me if I'm wrong, but you seem to be saying that the people who frequent your stores are a bunch of morons without an ounce of culture. Is that right?"

"Maggie! For Pete's sake!" Alex admonished anxiously. "What are you saying?"

Both Maggie and Clint ignored him. Seemingly fascinated by the belligerent thrust of her jaw and the challenging glitter in her blue eyes, Clint studied her closely for a long, tense moment.

"No, I'm not saying that at all," he responded quietly. "What I am saying is that I think we would benefit more from sponsoring a local sporting event, or an outdoorsman's show."

"And you, Henry? Do you agree with him?" Maggie demanded, switching her attention to the older man.

"Well, now, he does have a point." Henry pursed his lips and pulled thoughtfully at the waddle of skin beneath his chin. "The kind of shows he's talking about would draw the avid sportsman."

"That's true, but you should aim for a broader audience than just the macho male, mighty hunter, or dedicated jock," she argued, flicking Clint a dismissive look that clearly told in which category she had placed him. "A great many of your customers are desk-bound businessmen who play tennis and golf for exercise, weekend fishermen who just want a chance to get away from it all now and then, seasonal hunters who only go out once or twice a year, but spend a fortune when they do. In other words, Henry, your customers come from all walks of life and have widely divergent interests and educational backgrounds. Our program is designed to appeal to that broad spectrum."

Henry Burk's face wore a considering expression, his brows cocked high, creating furrows all the way up to the top of his bald head. He thought for a moment, then looked at his partner. "Well, Clint? What do you say to that?"

"I think the amount of business we derive from the occasional athlete or sportsman Maggie is speaking of is questionable. But even if she's right, there's still the problem of the time schedule." His gaze turned directly on her. The slight smile he gave was so smugly confident that she wanted to slap him. "Those tired businessmen you were talking about are seldom home at three in the afternoon."

The arrival of their food prevented Maggie from replying, and at Henry's suggestion the rest of the discussion was postponed until after they had eaten.

As she applied herself to the huge meal, Maggie was silent and thoughtful. She had deliberately avoided the question of the show's time slot because it was a valid point, one with which she happened to agree. For years she had been arguing with her boss, J. D. Grosseman, the station's general manager, that the show was being aired too early, but all her protests had been firmly dismissed.

Chewing absently on the delicious veal parmigiana,

Maggie wondered if the possibility of losing a major sponsor would be enough to convince J.D. to change his mind.

Throughout the meal Selene kept the men engaged in conversation on everything from the current economic climate to the new play opening at the Alley Theatre, while Maggie silently weighed her alternatives. By the time she'd finished her chocolate cake, her plan of attack was carefully thought out.

"What I'd like to propose, gentlemen," she announced as soon as the waiter had poured their coffee and retreated, "is that I have the show moved to the five-thirty time slot." The bold suggestion brought a gasp from Alex and a sharp look from Selene, but Maggie ignored them and pressed on doggedly. "I think you'll find there are definite advantages to being the lead-in to the six o'clock news. At that time of day the children are out playing baseball in the street and the breadwinner is ready to relax for a few minutes in front of the TV before dinner. Your adult audience should expand considerably. After the show has occupied that time slot for, say, a month to six weeks, I'll get our P.R. department to conduct a spot telephone survey. In it we'll be checking for three things: Is the man of the house watching? If so, does he shop at Sporting Chance? And what type of occupation does he have?" Maggie forced a confident smile to her lips and looked from one man to the other, holding her breath as she waited for their replies.

"That sounds fair to me," Henry said decisively. "How about you, Clint?"

Meeting the hard speculation in Clint's narrowed gaze, Maggie squirmed inwardly, but she refused to look away. For several tense moments their eyes locked in silent battle.

"All right," he said at last. "We'll try it Maggie's way

for now. Just as long as she realizes that no contract will be signed until after the survey, and then only if it comes up to expectations."

Dazed by the success of her reckless proposal, Maggie felt as though she were walking on air as they left the restaurant. She didn't even object when Clint cupped her elbow as they stepped through the door and started across the parking lot. It wasn't until they were almost to Selene's silvery-gray Cadillac that her euphoric bubble was burst by his whispered words in her ear.

"I hope you enjoy your reprieve, little Maggie," he taunted mockingly. "Because believe me, it won't last."

"Arrogant jock!"

Maggie's shoe hit the wall with a resounding thump. Another kick sent the other one sailing after it.

"Arrogant, skirt-chasing jock!" Storming across her office in stiff-legged fury, Maggie hissed the words that had been simmering in her mind since Clint had delivered his parting shot.

"Big, dumb, gristle-headed . . . *football player!*" She slammed her purse down onto the desk, then turned and began to pace the room, at last able to give vent to the flaming anger she had held tightly in check since the moment she walked into that restaurant and encountered Clint's mocking face.

Unwittingly, during the ride back to the station, Alex had fanned those flames even higher with his excited, nonstop praise of the man's prowess on the gridiron. Learning that for twelve years Clint had been the San Antonio Drovers' leading tight end had been the crowning blow as far as Maggie was concerned.

Selene, following closely behind, paused in the doorway just long enough to smile at Maggie's secretary, who was gaping at the sight of her diminutive boss stalking back and forth across her office in her stocking feet muttering a string of extremely uncomplimentary epithets.

With an imperious, "Hold her calls," Selene stepped into Maggie's office and shut the door. Taking the chair in front of the desk, she calmly withdrew a cigarette from her purse and lit it, watching her young friend with amused curiosity.

"I know you're not pleased with the situation, but don't you think you're overreacting just a bit?" she drawled as Maggie reached the far wall and whirled around.

"No I do not!" she spat emphatically, blue eyes blazing. "That man is impossible. I could have given him a hundred, *a thousand,* sound reasons why they should continue their sponsorship, and it wouldn't have made any difference. He's determined to get back at me for what happened over the weekend."

Selene's arched brows almost disappeared beneath the fringe of expertly dyed blond hair covering her forehead. "That sounds ominous . . . and fascinating," she murmured interestedly. "What exactly did happen?"

In pungent, colorful words, Maggie gave her a detailed account of her previous encounters with Henry's new partner. By the time she had finished Selene was howling.

"It's *not* funny, Selene!" Maggie snapped when her friend was forced to snatch a tissue from the box on the desk and dab at her eyes.

"Oh, Maggie, Maggie." Her name was choked out between hoots of laughter. "I've never known you to do anything halfway. Even your disasters are thorough. You don't humiliate just *any* man by walking in on him in the middle of a torrid love scene. Oh, no, not you. It has to be Henry's new partner. Then you proceed to ridicule his taste in women, rebuff his amorous advances, express disapproval of his life style, and sic your dog on him, all in the space of a few hours."

The laughing words extinguished the fire of Maggie's anger as effectively as a splash of cold water, and she halted in her tracks, her shoulders sagging. "I've really fouled things up, haven't I?" she sighed in a forlorn little voice.

Selene's face softened with fondness as she watched Maggie slump dejectedly into her chair. "Oh, I don't know. No doubt you injured his pride, and maybe even dented his ego a bit, but I don't think Clint's a vindictive man." Selene shook her head sadly. "What I can't understand is why you resisted him. I mean, darling, the man's a hunk. Why, if I were twenty years younger I'd be after him like a shot."

"Even if you dropped thirty years I'm afraid you still wouldn't be in the running, my friend," Maggie informed her dryly. "Clinton Rafferty's taste runs to very young, bubble-headed, busty blondes. Luckily, I don't qualify either."

"Are you trying to tell me you don't find that gorgeous man attractive?" Selene asked with a sly smile.

"Oh, I find him attractive all right." Maggie's mouth twisted into a wry grin. "I seem to have a weakness for big, good-looking womanizers. I think it must be a basic flaw in my character." The flippant remark was no sooner out than she sobered and added in a quiet, serious voice, "But weaknesses, once recognized, can be overcome."

For a long moment Selene eyed her narrowly. After one last draw on the cigarette, she crushed it out, blew a stream of smoke into the air, and tactfully changed the subject. "How, if I may be so bold as to ask, are you going to get J.D. to move the show to the five-thirty slot?''

Maggie grimaced. "I haven't the slightest idea. I made that suggestion in a moment of sheer panic. And at this moment I'd say my chances range from poor to zilch." Thrusting spread fingers through the silky brown hair, she pressed her palms against her temples and closed her eyes. "How do I get myself into these messes?" she groaned.

"Chin up, hon. If anyone can pull it off, you can. I've seen you knocked to your knees many times, but you always manage to pull yourself together and come up swinging." Hooking her purse strap over her shoulder, Selene stood up and headed for the door. "Just let me know when the change takes place."

The next morning, buoyed by Selene's encouragement, Maggie dressed in her most businesslike gray suit and rust silk blouse and marched into J.D. Grosseman's office to present her case.

Maggie liked J.D. and, on the whole, considered him to be a good boss, but to her way of thinking he had one glaring fault: he hated change and resisted it stubbornly. The draperies in his office were the same ones that had been installed twenty years ago when the station first opened. He had his shoes resoled until the top leather literally fell apart, and his ties were at least ten years behind the current fashion, which was fine, because his hair style was too. Unless he had a business appointment, he went to the same restaurant every day at the same time and, Maggie suspected, ordered the same thing. When his secretary of twelve years resigned to get married he viewed it as out and out desertion. Even to suggest a change in the program schedule was heresy.

"Dammit, Maggie! We've been all through this a

dozen times," he exploded the moment she broached the subject. "The show is doing well right where it is. And you know we've always had sitcom reruns in the five-to-six slot."

"I also know if we don't make this change you can kiss the Sporting Chance advertising money goodbye."

"Henry Burk wouldn't do that," J.D. scoffed. "Why he's been sponsoring 'Houston Today' since its debut." Brushing aside her claim with a complacent chuckle, he leaned back in his chair and chewed contentedly on his stub of a cigar.

"Maybe not, but his new partner, Clinton Rafferty, would."

Maggie's softly spoken words wiped the self-satisfied look from his face instantly. Sitting forward, J.D. gave her a beetling frown over the top of his wire-rimmed glasses. "Clinton Rafferty? The Clinton Rafferty who used to play for the San Antonio Drovers is Henry's new partner?"

"That's right. And he's adamant about the time change."

The cigar bobbed up and down as his teeth worried at it. He picked up a pencil and tapped the eraser end nervously against the desk pad. Maggie could almost hear the wheels turning in his head.

He looked up suddenly, frowning. "Isn't there any way you can talk him out of it?" he demanded sharply.

Maggie spread her hands wide and shrugged. "No. Either we move the show, or Clint and Henry pick up their marbles and play in someone else's yard."

J.D. cursed under his breath and flung the pencil aside.

Sensing that his resolve was weakening, Maggie pressed her advantage. "Come on, J.D., it's not that big a deal. In fact, we'll probably increase our viewing audience. Children don't watch TV at that time of day, and every person over the age of eighteen has seen each of those reruns at least twenty times. 'Houston Today' is fresh and new each day."

The look he gave her was one of grim reluctance, but after a moment he released a gusting sigh and growled, "Oh, all right! We'll give it a try. But I'm warning you, if this little plan doesn't work, I'm holding you personally responsible."

Exercising remarkable restraint, Maggie thanked him politely and hot-footed it out before he could change his mind. But when she walked into her own office and found Alex waiting for her she could no longer curb her delight. With a whoop of joy she threw herself into the startled man's arms.

"I did it! I did it! Beginning next Monday 'Houston Today' will be shown at five thirty!" she cried jubilantly.

"You're kidding!" Alex held her at arm's length and stared down at her, but gradually his goggled-eyed expression changed as he took in her beaming face and sparkling eyes, and with something akin to awe, he breathed, "You're *not* kidding!

"Maggie! Maggie! You little miracle worker, you did it!" he shouted suddenly, hugging her to him and whirling her around and around in a joyous dance. "I didn't think we had a chance of budging J.D., but I should have known better than to count you out."

When they finally came to a halt Maggie was flushed and laughing. "Well, don't forget, we've only fought half the battle," she reminded him, self-consciously pushing the wildly disordered hair away from her face. "If that survey doesn't come up to par, you and I both may be standing in the unemployment line, my friend."

"I refuse to even consider that possibility," he declared loftily. "And I think half a battle won rates a celebration. How does dinner and dancing at Renauldo's sound to you?"

"Sounds terrific."

Allison breezed into the study and plopped down in the chair opposite her father's desk. "Say, Dad, you ever been to a place called Renauldo's?" she asked innocently.

Clint looked up from the magazine he was reading and raised a brow. "A couple of times. Why?"

"Oh, I don't know. Just curious, I guess," she replied with a careless shrug. "I was just talking to Laura on the phone, and she said her mom was getting all dressed up to go there for dinner. I just wondered what it was like."

"It's very elegant, very nice. I'm sure Mrs. Trent will have an enjoyable evening."

"Yeah, I guess so," Allison agreed, in a voice that held just the barest trace of wistfulness. As quickly as she had settled in the chair she bounced right out again. "Oh, well, I guess I'd better hit the books. I've got tons of homework."

Clint sat perfectly still when she had gone, the magazine tossed aside and forgotten. His expression was pensive, searching, remote. Broodingly, he stared at the closed door for several minutes, then abruptly snatched up the phone and punched out a number.

"Hello, Lisa? Clint Rafferty. Listen, how would you feel about dinner at Renauldo's tonight?"

Out in the hallway, Allison smiled, pushed herself away from the door, and sauntered toward the stairs, humming softly, her fingertips stuck in the back pockets of her jeans.

Chapter Four

The world outside looked like black velvet sprinkled with diamonds. Perched atop a fifty-two-story building, the glass-walled restaurant gave an uninterrupted view, and it was difficult to tell where the canopy of stars left off and the lights of the sprawling city began. Maggie gazed dreamily at the sparkling display over Alex's shoulder as her feet followed his steps with effortless grace.

They always danced well together, but tonight Maggie felt as though she were floating on air. She had set herself a difficult goal and achieved it, and the heady feel of success had gone to her head like fine wine. She felt lightheaded. High. Invincible.

"You're looking mighty pleased with yourself tonight," Alex teased gently.

Tilting her head back, Maggie smiled up at him. "I *am* pleased with myself. Winning over the powers that be does that to me."

Alex executed an intricate step, deftly maneuvering

them out of the way of a couple who seemed to be blundering around the floor in a controlled stagger rather than dancing.

Maggie found the sudden move exhilarating and laughed gaily.

The husky, vibrant sound drew an appreciative look from Alex. "Have I told you recently that you're one fantastic lady?" he asked with only a touch of laughter in his voice.

"No, but feel free."

Smiling, Maggie let her eyes run over his face, noting, one by one, the perfectly chiseled nose, the sculptured masculine lips, the vivid blue eyes, the lean cheeks, and the strong jaw. There was no doubt about it: Alex Crenna was an extremely handsome man. He was also a very nice man. So why, she wondered abstractedly, wasn't she attracted to him? She enjoyed his company immensely, but all she had ever felt for him, all she would ever feel for him, was a sort of warm fondness. It was puzzling.

The music ended, and when it was announced that the band would take a short break Alex guided Maggie back toward their table.

They were halfway there when Maggie's eyes locked with a pair of familiar green ones, and her heart leaped right up into her throat.

Oh no! Not Clinton Rafferty. Why did he have to show up just when I was feeling so great?

With a sinking feeling in the pit of her stomach, Maggie realized they would have to pass right by his table to get to theirs, and for a moment her steps faltered. Then, meeting his taunting look, she tilted her chin and moved forward. She would not let Clint Rafferty spoil her evening.

He rose as they drew level with his table. "Hello, Maggie. Alex. This is a pleasant surprise."

"Clint! Nice to see you again." Alex accepted Clint's handshake and returned the greeting with obvious pleasure. Maggie barely managed a frosty smile and a stiff nod.

Not in the least put off by her aloofness, Clint introduced them to his date, a red-haired young beauty named Lisa Brady, who was prettily flustered at meeting a local celebrity like Alex. Maggie she ignored.

As soon as the greetings were exchanged, Maggie murmured a polite banality and began to edge away, but Clint's, "Why don't you two join us for a drink?" halted her in her tracks.

Maggie's horrified gaze flew to Alex, but he was smiling broadly at the other couple and didn't see the silent plea in her eyes. Frantic, she turned back to Clint and opened her mouth to refuse, but she wasn't quick enough.

"Why, we'd be happy to," Alex accepted with a beaming smile. "I'll just run over and get Maggie's purse and shawl from our table."

Maggie stood helplessly and watched him walk away. When this evening is over I'm personally going to strangle Alex Crenna, she vowed silently.

Meeting the triumphant amusement in her host's eyes she gave him a cool smile and sat down in the chair he held out for her, mentally kicking herself for being a fool. She should have known that Alex would be eager to ingratiate himself with the man. If she'd had a lick of sense she would have cut and run the moment she saw him.

For the next half-hour Maggie struggled to ignore the long, intent looks she was receiving from Clint and the pressure of his knee against hers beneath the table. She tried several times to strike up a conversation with Lisa, but the young woman merely passed off her opening gambits with an irritated look and a mumbled reply, then immediately turned her attention back to Alex. After a while Maggie gave up and quietly sipped her drink while the others talked.

Feeling Clint's eyes on her again she fidgeted in her seat and stared at her white wine while nervous fingers rotated the stemglass. When a hard, masculine hand closed around her forearm she jumped as though she'd received a jolt of electricity.

"Dance with me, Maggie."

The softly spoken command brought Maggie's head up, and she found herself gazing into a pair of mesmerizing green eyes that glittered with challenge and amusement, and something else she didn't care to analyze.

"I . . . uh . . ." Her mind groped for a diplomatic way of refusing. Dancing with Clint would undoubtedly be a pleasurable and exhilarating experience, but she had a strong suspicion it would also be dangerous to her emotional health. She found him too darned attractive for her own good. Aggravating, arrogant, opinionated, and a heartbreaking swine . . . but attractive all the same. Definitely a man to avoid at all costs. Yet she couldn't just bluntly refuse him. He was, after all, one of the show's sponsors, or soon would be at any rate.

Smiling politely, she started to plead fatigue when all at once the band switched from a soft, dreamy tune to hard rock.

Maggie paused and glanced at the gyrating couples on the dance floor, then at the large man by her side, and slowly the corners of her mouth curled upward.

"Why thank you, Clint. I'd love to dance," she accepted with honeyed sweetness and, as docile as a lamb, allowed him to lead her from the table. By the time they stepped onto the dance floor Maggie's blue eyes were sparkling with devilish anticipation.

But any hope she had harbored that Clint would be awkward or ill at ease was quickly squashed when he began to dance, moving with a lithe, easy grace that was unusual in a man his size.

For a moment surprise and grudging admiration mingled on Maggie's face as she watched him, but then the music took over and she abandoned herself to the pulsating rhythm.

With each sinuous movement the ice blue, crepe de chine dress flowed against her petite body like water, molding and caressing the curves it covered. The straight, side-slit skirt showed flashes of shapely limbs and hugged undulating hips lovingly, while beneath the blousoned, strapless top, firm, uptilted breasts swayed in subtle enticement.

Maggie closed her eyes and lost herself in the pounding explosion of sound, letting it throb through her, becoming an extension of it, moving with an exquisite, sensuous grace. Every cell in her body responded to the heavy, primitive beat. From the top of her swinging brown hair to the soles of her dainty feet she was one continuous flow of fluid rhythm.

Slowly she lifted her lids and found Clint dancing in front of her, only a few feet away, and smiled at him dreamily, still caught up in the spell of the wild music. He watched her, not missing a single, provocative sway of her lithe body, his eyes a dark, mysterious green.

When at last the song ended in a crashing crescendo Maggie's shoulders sagged, and a breathless laugh escaped her as she looked up at Clint. "Thanks, that was great." With a smile, she turned and started for their table.

"Oh, no you don't, you little devil." Clint chuckled

wickedly, pulling her to him as the band began to play a slow, romantic ballad. "You still owe me a dance. That workout didn't count."

He wrapped both arms around her waist and brought her snugly against him, fitting their bodies together with shattering intimacy. Maggie's heart was already beating fast from the exertion of dancing, but now it took off at a snare drum roll.

Trying to put more space between them, Maggie pressed her palms against his chest and leaned back, realizing too late that she was only succeeding in bringing their lower bodies in closer contact. She darted a quick, reproachful glance up at Clint and immediately wished she hadn't. His slow, sexy smile did crazy things to her.

"Were you deliberately trying to drive me out of my mind, or do you always dance with such abandon?" he asked huskily.

Maggie slanted him a cool look and said nothing.

"Honey, do you have any idea what it does to a man to watch that sexy little body move like that?" He pulled her closer. Bending his head, he nibbled a provocative line across her bare shoulder and up the side of her neck, then nuzzled her ear, his teeth nipping gently on the velvety lobe. "I wanted to throw you down and make passionate love to you right here on the floor. *That* is what you do to a man."

Maggie shivered violently. Whether it was in reaction to his evocative words or to the hand that slid boldly downward to cup the firm flesh of her buttock, she didn't know. Desire coursed hotly through her veins, its intensity stunning her and turning her knees to mush. All the needs, all the longings that had lain dormant for years now sprang into clamoring life in response to the tactile exploration of his hands, the feel of his hard, muscular body pressed so intimately to hers. "I

. . . you . . . you shouldn't say that," she choked as she tried to fight her way through the morass of feelings that threatened to swamp her common sense.

"Why not? It's true," he whispered with a wicked chuckle.

His warm breath skated across her cheek, raising gooseflesh over her arms and shoulders. The low, husky pitch of his voice was a subtle seduction. "No. . . ."

"Yes. You're a lovely, desirable woman, little Maggie. I've thought so since the moment I saw you." As if to prove his words, his hands spread over her back and hips to mold her to him, the evidence of his arousal making her breathtakingly aware of just how desirable he found her. "And don't try to tell me the feeling isn't mutual, because I won't buy it." Softly, maddeningly, his tongue traced an intricate pattern over the delicate skin just behind her ear. "I can feel you trembling, sweetheart," he murmured huskily.

It was useless to deny it. She *was* trembling. She had never felt this drawn to any man before. Larry, with his most passionate lovemaking, had never aroused in her this deep, almost intolerable longing for fulfillment. "That . . . that's b–beside the point," she stammered in a desperate attempt to stem the thrilling sensations welling up inside her. *For God's sake, get a grip on yourself Maggie! You're a grown woman, not some love-struck teenager.* "This is ridiculous. We're . . . we're business associates, a–and parents of young . . . im–impressionable girls."

"We're also a man and woman who are attracted to each other. Why fight it? Have dinner with me tomorrow, Maggie," he urged as he nuzzled her neck. "Give us a chance to get to know one another."

His tongue explored each convoluted swirl in her ear,

and Maggie shivered. She was tempted. Oh, yes, she was tempted. He felt so good. Smelled so good.

But even as her resolve began to waver, Maggie looked dreamily over Clint's shoulder and her eyes came to rest on Lisa Brady's flame-red head.

The mist of desire that surrounded her evaporated instantly. How could she have forgotten, even for a brief moment, that Clint was here with another woman? And that there was little doubt as to how the evening would end for them.

Maggie clamped her jaws together, the muscles in her cheeks taut and strained as she pictured all that red hair spread out on a pillow and Lisa's arms and long slender legs wrapped around Clint's naked body. Hating the sudden painful tightness that twisted her insides, Maggie shook her head, banishing the image from her mind. But no sooner had it faded than another took its place, only this time the woman in Clint's arms was the beautiful, busty blonde he had been wrestling with on the sofa just a few nights ago.

Maggie ground her teeth until they ached. If he thought he was going to sweet-talk her into joining his harem, he had another think coming. Just because her body turned to Silly Putty every time she looked at him, she didn't have to commit emotional suicide. And that was exactly what she would be doing if she let herself get involved with Clint. The pain and humiliation she had suffered over Larry's infidelities had been bad enough, but some deep-seated instinct warned her that Clint could not only break her heart, he could destroy her very soul.

Stiffening in his arms, Maggie tilted her head back and gave him a disdainful look, her eyes narrowed, a small, cool smile curving her lips. "This whole conversation is absurd. I have no intention of getting to know you one whit better than I already do, Mr. Rafferty. On the one hand, we're business associates. On the other, we're casual acquaintances. And that's exactly how things are going to remain."

The music ended, and without another word Maggie turned and started to walk away, but Clint's hand on her wrist stopped her.

"Just tell me one thing," he commanded in a low tone that sent a tiny frisson up her spine. "Is it because of Crenna?"

"What?"

"Is he the reason you're fighting so hard to keep the Sporting Chance sponsorship? The reason you won't go out with me?"

"What?" Maggie repeated in open-mouthed astonishment.

"I want to know if you're lovers."

Eyes round, Maggie stared up at him for a full five seconds before she finally found her voice and snapped, "No! Of course not. Alex and I are good friends who enjoy each other's company, that's all. Not that my relationship with Alex is any of your business," she added hastily, mentally kicking herself for answering his question in the first place.

A slow grin split his face. "Good. That's all I wanted to know," he said in a voice that oozed male satisfaction and made Maggie's palm itch to slap him.

Fuming, she pivoted on her heel.

Following slowly, Clint watched her stalk back to the table, noting the enticing movement of her hips, the proud, stiff carriage that telegraphed her anger, the haughty tilt of her chin, the silky swing of her shining hair. *God, she's adorable when she's angry. Hell, face it, man. She's adorable period.*

The admission brought a slow smile to Clint's lips. Since the moment he had met her, thoughts of Maggie

Trent had been playing merry hell with his peace of mind. Just being around her excited him, made him feel eager and alive and filled him with an irrational joy that sent his spirits soaring to a level they hadn't reached in years. He was thirty-six years old, but around Maggie he felt about twenty: hot and lusty and ready to take on the world.

Maybe I've been wrong, he thought hopefully, as his long legs closed the gap between them. Maybe, just maybe, if you're very lucky, you do get a second chance.

Clint reached the table just as Maggie leaned over the back of her chair and picked up her purse and shawl. "I'm ready to leave, Alex," she announced in a voice that brooked no argument, and Alex looked up, his eyes wide with surprise.

He opened his mouth to speak but thought better of it after a second look at Maggie's set expression. Ever the diplomat, Alex expressed his pleasure at meeting Lisa, thanked Clint for the drink, and with a pleasant smile wished them good night and ushered a stony-faced Maggie toward the door.

An hour later, angrily pacing the floor of her room, Maggie suddenly realized that she had no idea what, if anything, she had said to Alex on the way home, or if she'd even told him good night.

"That's what happens when you let your attraction to a man get in the way of your better judgment," she muttered in disgust. "It rattles not only your libido but your brain as well."

The lace edge of her peach nightgown fluttered around her ankles as she stalked to the dresser and snatched up her hairbrush. Attacking her shining smooth hair with vicious strokes, she snarled darkly at her reflection, "Why do you let that muscle-bound Romeo upset you? So he's charming, good-looking,

and sexy. So what? He's also one of the show's
sponsors, Allison's father, and a conceited, arrogant,
lecherous jock to boot. All of which spells nothing but
trouble. And anyway, he's probably just bored with his
youthful bedmates and looking for a temporary diversion."

Maggie slammed the brush down on the dressing
table and spun on her heel. "Which I'll be damned if I'll
supply," she vowed as she stormed across the room and
yanked back the covers on her bed.

Sleep was a fitful affair that night, punctuated by
disturbing dreams in which Larry's face kept merging
into Clint's and Clint's into Larry's.

When her alarm went off at five the next morning
Maggie's arm flew out from under the cover, and the
palm of her hand whacked it into silence. Wooden-
headed and moaning, she hauled herself out of bed and
pulled on a shapeless gray flannel sweatsuit and a pair
of thick-soled running shoes. With her hip propped
against the dresser, she dozed her way through a
perfunctory hairbrushing and tied the shining mass
back with a scarf, then, opening her eyes to mere slits,
turned and stumbled sleepily out of the house.

The sky had just begun to lighten to a pearly gray
when she reached the park, two blocks away. Setting
her mouth in a grim line, she pumped her knees up and
down for a few minutes to warm up her muscles, then
took off at a determined jog.

Briefly a bird trilled its morning song from a nearby
tree, then there were only the sounds of grit underfoot
and her huffing breath to counterpoint the still of the
morning. The trees and shrubs on either side of the
path were laden with dew and strung with gossamer
webs to which droplets of water clung like tiny crystal
beads. The leaves had just begun to change color, and

the October morning held a damp chill which hadn't been present only a week ago.

By the time she had circled the park once Maggie was greedily sucking huge gulps of the cool, refreshing air into her tortured lungs. Left, right. Left, right, she silently chanted, urging her exhausted limbs onward. Her heart was pumping ninety to nothing, and her thigh bones felt as though they would push right up through the tops of her hips, but still she forced one foot in front of the other.

Head down, she was watching the rhythmic slap of her feet against the ground when suddenly they were joined by another, larger pair. In her peripheral vision all she saw was a large, extremely fit masculine body, bare except for brief red athletic shorts with a white stripe down the side.

Maggie kept her head down and continued to jog.

For five minutes she alternately slowed down and speeded up, but the size twelve shoes stayed with her, causing her temper to simmer. Finally, in no mood to put up with an early morning masher, she snarled, "Get away from me!"

"Charming. Has anyone ever told you, little Maggie, that your manners are appalling?"

Clint's deep baritone brought Maggie's head up sharply, and for just an instant she stumbled. Her wide, startled eyes met a smug smile and glinting green eyes. "What are you doing here?" she demanded rudely as her feet regained the even rhythm.

"Now is that any way to talk? After I've searched all over this park trying to find you?"

She stumbled again. "Trying to find me? How did you know I'd be here?"

"Oh, Allison mentioned that you jog here every morning, and since I run a couple of miles every day, too, I didn't see any reason why we shouldn't keep each other company.''

Maggie stared at him disbelievingly. She could think of any number of reasons, but before she could state one he added, "If I had known you liked to jog I would have joined you before now.''

"Like, ha!" Maggie slanted him a look of pure disgust. "I hate every miserable minute of it.''

"Then why do you do it?'' he asked, looking comically bewildered.

"Because, in case you haven't noticed, I like to eat. It's either diet or exercise, and there's no way I'm going to go hungry." She eyed him irritably. *Why was it that she was huffing like a locomotive and he wasn't even breathing hard?*

"Ah, I see. To tell you the truth, I had noticed that you have a rather . . . ah . . . large appetite for such a little bitty thing.''

The reference to her size made her grind her teeth, but she said nothing. Keeping her eyes straight ahead, she plodded on.

The tingle that spread over Maggie's skin had nothing to do with exertion. She was intensely, uncomfortably aware of the man at her side. She could feel the heat from his body, smell the warm male scent of him. Sweat glistened on tanned skin, sharply defining every smooth flex and shift of rock-hard muscles, making Maggie acutely, painfully aware of his potent masculinity.

What was he doing, tracking her down at the crack of dawn like this? Had she, by refusing him, become a challenge? *Heaven help me, I hope not,* she thought desperately. She wasn't sure she had the strength to resist him if he pursued her in earnest.

They had made another complete circle of the park before he spoke again, and when he did his voice no longer held even a trace of laughter.

"You know, Maggie, I applaud your efforts at physical fitness, but I really don't think it's safe for you to be jogging alone at this time of the morning. There are some real wierdos in this world. Anything could happen to you."

"Oh, but I'm not alone," Maggie assured him with a sweet smile. "Just watch this." Without breaking stride, she stuck two fingers in her mouth and emitted a piercing, totally unladylike whistle.

"Awwwww, jeeeeez," Clint groaned a few seconds later when Tiny came bounding out of the small woods in the middle of the park, barking his fool head off. Maggie had run a half dozen steps before she realized that Clint was no longer with her.

Glancing back over her shoulder she burst out laughing, then made a quick U-turn and jogged back.

At the first sight of Tiny, Clint had snagged a low-hanging tree branch and hoisted himself out of reach. He now sat astraddle the branch, looking down at the gamboling dog with a gimlet eye. Tiny was jumping and barking beneath him, acting for all the world like a hound who had treed a possum.

Jogging in place, Maggie grinned up at him. "Why, Mr. Rafferty. Don't tell me you're afraid of Tiny? He's an absolute lamb, I assure you."

Clint shot the "lamb" a baleful look. "You'll pardon me if I doubt that, won't you," he drawled, fingering the three neat stitches above his left brow.

Again Maggie's rich peal of laughter lifted through the trees. When it died away she issued a sharp command that brought the excited dog to heel. She came to a halt and struggled for a moment to subdue her labored breathing, sucking in great draughts of air, chest heaving. Standing with hands on hips, she stuck out her lower jaw and blew upward, momentarily lifting the stray wisps of hair away from her sticky forehead. Finally she looked up at Clint. Her eyes were brimming with unholy mirth. "Oh, for heaven's sake, come on down and let me introduce you," she ordered in teasing reproach. "That way Tiny will know you're a friend."

Frowning, Clint cautiously did as she instructed, keeping a wary eye on Tiny all the while. When he reached the ground she took his hand and, ignoring his instinctive tug of resistance, extended it toward the dog.

Nose quivering, Tiny sniffed first the fingers, then the palm, and then proceeded to anoint the whole thing with a huge, slobbering lick.

"See. I told you he was harmless," Maggie said smugly as a look of pleased surprise slowly spread over Clint's face.

He bent over and fondled the dog's great head. "No animal this size is completely harmless, Maggie. As I know to my cost. What on earth prompted you to buy such a monster?"

"Can you think of a better protector for two females on their own?"

Clint laughed. "No. Come to think of it, I can't."

After giving the dog one final pat, he straightened up and planted his hands on his hips, then thoroughly confounded her by saying, "So, what time shall I pick you up tonight? I thought we'd have dinner at Tony's and maybe go to that new coffee house that opened up on Westheimer."

Maggie's jaw dropped. *"What? Are you crazy?"* she shrieked when she regained control of her tongue. "Didn't you hear a word I said last night? I will not—"

The angry spate of words was cut off as Clint's lips closed over hers. Swallowing the strangled sound of outrage that issued from her throat, and ignoring her frantic struggles, he slipped one arm around her waist and the other beneath her bottom and lifted her high against his chest.

As their overheated bodies seemed to fuse together, Maggie's struggles came to an abrupt halt, her heart slamming against her ribs. She was sure her damp sweatsuit was steaming.

His lips explored hers leisurely, sipping, tasting, devouring her with a sweet restrained hunger that took her breath away and sent liquid fire racing through her veins. Slipping quickly past her lips, his warm tongue swept over the curving roof of her mouth, then skated over her teeth to test the delicate membrane on the inside of her cheek. Even as she told herself that she must stop him, that he was too dangerous, too attractive, and much too good at this, her hands slid slowly around his neck, her fingers clutching the thick hair at his nape as her own tongue hesitantly responded to the persistent probing.

Oh, Maggie, you're such a fool. This man's no good, and you know it.

But her silent scolding went unheeded as Clint's mouth and hands continued their magic.

The kiss grew deeper, more intimate, more demanding, until finally, with a small whimper, Maggie gave up all attempts at resistance and melted against him, her fingers flexing convulsively in his hair.

Leaning his back against the tree, Clint braced himself with his feet wide apart, and Maggie lay against him, her legs dangling between his. Freed of the need to support her so completely, his arm left her waist and both hands cupped her bottom, pressing her provocatively against his aroused body.

Every nerve, every cell in her body seemed to have sprung into tingling life. She was aware of the cool, sweat-dampened shirt against her back, the sizzling heat across her front where their yearning flesh strained to overcome the thin cloth barrier. She was aware of the labored harshness of Clint's breathing, the slam of his heart against her breast.

Clint took her lower lip into his mouth and sucked gently, and Maggie shivered, going suddenly boneless. When his hand slipped under her shirt and glided upward to press against the side of her breast she hadn't the strength or the desire to stop him. Lightly, maddeningly, his fingertips traced around the lower edge of her lacy bra, trailing ripples of fire across her back. Then suddenly the clasp between her shoulder blades was released. A moment later his hand slipped between them and his fingers found her freed breasts. Caressing gently, his fingertips teased the pouting nipples with a feathery touch.

Maggie moaned softly into his mouth. A small part of her brain still urged retreat, but she ignored the warning. His touch was so tender, so alluring, so wonderfully seductive.

All at once the ribald whistles and catcalls of two grinning youths jogging by on the narrow path made them shockingly aware that they were in plain view in a public park.

Mortified almost to the point of tears, her face flaming a brilliant crimson, Maggie jerked free of the ardent kiss and struggled against the steely arms that held her.

Clint suffered no such reaction. The lascivious grin he turned on the two hecklers made theirs look perfectly innocent.

Maggie glared indignantly and hissed, "Put me down this very minute, you oaf!"

He complied, letting her slide slowly, erotically against his body.

The moment her feet touched solid ground, Maggie stumbled backward and fumbled urgently to refasten the clasp on her bra. Still trembling and wondering what on earth had possessed her to let things go so far, she could only stare at him, her face taut with anger and humiliation.

Clint remained where he was. Crossing his arms over his chest, he bent one knee, propped the sole of his jogging shoe against the tree trunk, and watched her. The hot look in his eyes raised gooseflesh on Maggie's skin and made her more tinglingly aware of him than if he had reached out and touched her.

An involuntary shiver rippled through her, and his grin returned.

"Now, then, what time do you want me to pick you up tonight, little Maggie?"

She gaped at him. What did it take to get through to this man?

"I said I'm not going out with you. Not tonight. Not ever. Get that through your head, Rafferty!"

His slow grin was devastating. "One thing I learned playing football, little one, was not to give up. Not until that last second ticks off the clock. And you and I are just a couple of minutes into the first quarter."

"This is *not* a game, Clint!"

"I'm glad you realize that."

Maggie made a low sound of pure frustration, then closed her eyes and counted to ten. Somehow, some way, she had to make him see reason. "Look, Clint," she began with strained patience. "Surely you can understand why any sort of . . . of . . . personal involvement between us is out of the question. When it ended, not only would it put an intolerable strain on our business relationship, but both Laura and Allison would be hurt."

"You sound sure it will end."

"Of course it will end."

"Oh, I don't know." He considered her unhurriedly,

from the top of her head down over the shapeless gray sweatsuit to the scruffy running shoes. His smile both teased and tempted. "What if we fall madly in love and decide to get married?"

Maggie threw up her hands in disgust. "I give up! If you're not going to take me seriously, what's the use."

"But I intend to take you seriously, Maggie." His voice was low, silky, seductive, his heavy-lidded gaze burning with unspoken promise. "In fact, I'll take you any way I can get you."

"Oh!" Maggie gasped, her eyes wide. "Oh you . . . you . . . oh!" To her utter dismay she felt her body respond to the husky sensuality in his words. Held captive by the sexual tension that crackled in the air between them, she stared at him, trembling with a confusing, frustrating mixture of excitement and anger.

But it was her anger that was fed by the wolfish glint in his green eyes and the slow, knowing smile that stretched his sensual mouth, and for the first time since she was sixteen years old Maggie was consumed with the urge to scream and stamp her foot. It took every ounce of will power she possessed to control it.

She clinched her jaw and looked around wildly for Tiny. Spying him chasing a squirrel through the trees a little distance away, she emitted a shrill whistle, then, with one last withering glare at the maddening man leaning indolently against the tree, spun on her heel and took off across the park toward her home, praying fervently that her shaking legs would hold her.

Damn the man! What made him think he could just barge into her life and turn it upside down? She wouldn't allow it! She was perfectly happy as she was. When and if she wanted another man in her life, it certainly wouldn't be the likes of Clinton Rafferty. She wasn't *that* much of a fool.

Maggie glanced back over her shoulder and saw that

he was still where she had left him. Exuding a loose-limbed, unself-conscious grace, he stood with one hand braced against the tree, the other resting on his out-thrust hip, and watched her, a confident, infuriating grin splitting his face.

Anger brought renewed strength to her legs, and Maggie picked up her pace, determinedly ignoring the burning pain that seared her tortured lungs every time she sucked in a gulp of air. Okay, so his kisses did knock the props out from under her, she conceded with grudging self-honesty. So what? Big deal! There were probably hundreds, *thousands* of men out there who could affect her the same way. And anyway, with all those young girls fawning all over him what did Clint want with her? A drop of sweat trickled its way down her spine, and Maggie glanced down at her shapeless attire, her mouth firming into a thin line. And if he just *had* to grab her and kiss her, why in heaven's name did he always do it when she was smelling like a goat? she thought angrily. The man was either kinky or a slob or his sense of smell had been ruined by too many years spent in a locker room.

Whatever, she was going to have to steer clear of him. She wasn't about to jeopardize her career or her emotional well-being over a man like Clint. She'd learned her lesson.

Tiny came loping up, giving her a doggy grin, his tongue lolling out of the side of his mouth. She shot him a disgusted look and muttered, "Where were you when I needed you, you wretched beast?"

Tiny barked joyfully.

Chapter Five

Maggie groaned when she approached the park entrance the next morning. She couldn't believe it! He was there again!

She had gone to work the day before determined to put the aggravating man out of her mind, only to spend the entire day vacillating between dreamy distraction and snappish irritability. After a restless night she had awakened this morning feeling about as cheerful as a grizzly with an impacted tooth. The sight of Clint leaning nonchalantly against a lamppost didn't improve her disposition one iota.

To her disgust, Tiny raced ahead to greet him, licking his hand slavishly and whining.

"Miserable, disloyal creature," Maggie grumbled to herself. "Some help you are."

As she drew near, Clint straightened away from the post and grinned. "Morning, little one," he greeted casually, with a total disregard for her furious expression. "All set to do a few miles?"

"What are you doing here, Rafferty?" she demanded rudely. "Don't you hear well? I told you yesterday I have no intention of becoming involved with you."

Standing with his feet braced apart, hands on his hips, Clint heaved a sigh and shook his head. "Ask anyone you know, and I dare you to come up with one person who would classify jogging at dawn as 'getting involved.'"

"I still don't want you here."

He raised both brows. "This *is* a public park, you know."

It was a valid point, which only made Maggie angrier. Unable to come up with a suitably cutting reply, she pressed her lips into a thin line, shot him a scorching glare, and took off down the path. I'll just pretend he isn't here, she vowed silently as he fell in step beside her. He can follow me around this path until his tongue drags the ground, but I'm not going to speak to him!

"You know, you remind me a lot of my mother," Clint said conversationally, ignoring the fact that *she* was pointedly ignoring *him*. "Oh, not in looks or size." He chuckled softly and let his eyes slide over her petite body. "Mom would make two of you," he informed her. "But she was a feisty, independent, determined woman in her younger days. Hell, she still is, for that matter." When Maggie made no comment he added, "My dad died when I was seven and my brothers were five and three. She raised us alone, sometimes even working two jobs, just to keep us all together. She's a remarkable lady. You'll like her. And I guarantee she'll like you."

I'm not listening to this, Maggie told herself stubbornly. I'm not listening at all.

From the corner of her eye she saw Clint give her a long, intent look, but she kept her eyes straight ahead and plodded along at a steady pace.

"Growing up, my brothers and I were constantly into mischief in one form or another, but Mom just seemed to take it all in stride," he continued in the same conversational vein. "Looking back on it, I don't see how she kept her sanity."

During the next four circuits of the park Maggie made a discovery: It was extremely difficult, if not downright impossible, to give a man the cold shoulder when he was reminiscing about his mother and the exploits of his childhood.

By the time they had begun the last lap of the park he was telling a hilarious tale of the time he tied an old sheet around his younger brother's neck, Superman fashion, then tossed him out of a tree, certain he would fly. Luckily he landed in a brush pile and ended up with only a scratched up face and a few bruises.

"While I, on the other hand," Clint declared ruefully, "had to eat standing up for three days, after the walloping Mom gave me."

Maggie was hard pressed to contain the laughter that threatened to erupt from her throat. Darn the man! He had no business making her laugh! And you, Maggie Trent, have no business listening to him, she scolded severely.

When at last they had completed her usual number of laps and returned to the starting point, Maggie came to a weary halt and scooped up her towel from the bench where she had left it. Panting heavily, she mopped the sweat from her face and neck while her pounding heart gradually slowed. Clint she ignored.

"You know, Maggie, Allison and I drive up to Dallas fairly often to visit my mother. We'd like for you and Laura to join us sometime."

Maggie lifted her stunned face from the thick folds of the towel and stared at him. "I don't believe this," she choked incredulously, forgetting her vow of silence. "One minute you're attacking my show and threatening to sabotage it and my career by taking away your sponsorship, and the next you're trying to start something between us. What are you? Some kind of nut? This whole situation is impossible!"

"It's not impossible at all," he disputed forcefully. "I admit I have serious doubts about how our advertising money is being spent, but that has nothing to do with the attraction I feel for you. We're two mature adults. I see no reason why we can't keep the business and personal sides of our lives separate."

She blinked and shook her head, dazed. "It can't be done."

He stared back at her, a slow grin spreading over his face. "Wanna bet?"

Maggie lounged back in her chair, her stockinged feet propped on an open desk drawer. Occasionally she darted a glance at the TV monitor on the corner of her desk to check the show's progress, but her attention always returned quickly to the official bio she was studying. A smile curved her mouth as she read the vital statistics and the thoroughly intriguing but highly improbable background material on Nick Lawson, the young actor who was being promoted by his studio as the next Robert Redford.

Unclipping the glossy color photo from the back of the typed pages, Maggie chewed absently on the eraser end of her pencil and studied the handsome face that smiled back at her. Dark brown eyes, wheat-colored hair, and deeply tanned skin drew the eye like a magnet. In addition there was a beautifully modeled, slightly off-center nose, a strong jaw, and a delightfully wicked smile that revealed the whitest, most even teeth she had ever seen outside a toothpaste ad.

Despite all the Hollywood hype, Maggie had to admit that the young man definitely had that elusive something it took to attain stardom. In addition, she knew that Nick Lawson was thoroughly likable.

A little over two years before, when still a bit player, he had appeared on the show, and his unassuming manner had made him an instant hit with the entire crew. Maggie wondered briefly if the phenomenal success he had enjoyed in the last few months had altered his personality. She doubted it, since he had agreed so readily to appear on the show, even though he was now starring in his second major motion picture, which was to begin shooting in Houston in a few days.

Tossing the folder onto her desk, Maggie stretched sinuously, lifting her arms high above her head and pointing her toes. She relaxed with a sigh then, smiling, reached over and penciled in Nick's name on the taping schedule. She was looking forward to seeing him again.

A few minutes later, while Alex was skillfully wrapping up the show, Maggie was deeply engrossed in a production costs report. The credits had barely started rolling across the monitor screen when the phone rang. She reached out a hand and picked up the receiver without taking her eyes from the computer print out sheet.

"Maggie Trent speaking."

"An opera star, for God's sake! How many men do you think would sit still for that caterwauling?"

Maggie's eyes didn't falter once as they continued down the column of figures. She'd been expecting the call. "In this city? Oh, I'd say several thousand," she replied calmly. "At least, that's what the P.R. man for the Houston Grand Opera tells me. And it isn't caterwauling. Misha Kantrell happens to be one of Europe's leading sopranos. We were lucky she agreed to appear."

"Lucky, hell!" Clint snapped scathingly. "When she hit that high note every dog for three blocks around started howling. My ears will never be the same. And I don't care what some sissy with the opera says, that kind of so-called singing doesn't sell flyrods and tennis rackets."

And I suppose the nasal twang of country-western does, Maggie fumed silently.

"Look, Clint," she began with strained patience. "I realize that opera is probably not the favorite form of entertainment among macho male types, but Ms. Kantrell has been booked on the show for over a month. Long before you came on the scene. We simply could not cancel at the last minute. Anyway, we balanced her appearance with that physical fitness expert."

"Which was the only thing that made today's show bearable," he muttered.

Maggie cupped her forehead with her hand and moved the tips of her fingers and thumb over her temples in a circular motion. She was heartily sick of these daily bellyaching sessions. Lately her most cherished fantasy was one in which she told Clint Rafferty exactly what he could do with his sponsorship . . . in graphic and colorful terms. In fact, even now the words hovered on the tip of her tongue.

In an effort to contain them she took a deep breath and began counting, but before she reached five Clint added sarcastically, "Just to save us both the trouble, suppose you tell me what wonderful surprise you have in store for tomorrow."

Eight . . . nine . . . ten. Eyes closed, Maggie mentally ticked off the numbers, then forced out between clenched teeth, "Tomorrow we'll have Keith Lerner, the young man who circumnavigated the globe alone when he was only seventeen. He's on a cross-country tour, promoting his book about the trip."

"And?"

"And we'll have Dr. Norman Hallet, a noted specialist in child rearing."

"Ah, now there's a riveting subject for a man."

"Yes, isn't it," Maggie agreed sweetly, ignoring his heavy sarcasm. "I was sure you'd see the need for Dr. Hallet's expertise, what with all the single parents in today's society. You and I, in fact, are perfect examples. And I know how concerned you are about Allison's happiness." A smug smile pulled at Maggie's mouth. She had him there. She could almost hear his teeth grinding.

The silence stretched out for several seconds. "When will you be finished with that survey?" Clint demanded gruffly.

"The figures are being compiled now. We should have the results by next Monday."

"Good. I can hardly wait to see how you like the taste of crow."

"What do you mean, crow? Now look here, Clint . . . ! Clint?"

When the receiver began to buzz, Maggie jerked it away from her ear and stared at it in astonishment. He had hung up on her!

With a strangled sound, Maggie slammed the instrument back into its cradle so hard that it jumped right out again. She glared at it as though it were responsible for all her troubles, then, after replacing it with only slightly less force, she jerked up out of her chair and stalked across to the window. Wrapping her arms across her midriff, she cupped her elbows and rubbed them while her eyes absently followed the steady stream of traffic on the freeway a few blocks away.

Unconsciously, her toes curled into the plush carpet underfoot.

Maggie shook her head. It was hard to believe that arrogant, sarcastic devil was the same man who persisted in following her around the jogging path every morning, flirting outrageously and keeping up a constant flow of lighthearted banter. Talk about your Jeckyll and Hyde!

If his aim was to keep her off balance, he'd certainly succeeded. Her emotional equilibrium had been upset for the past three weeks, ever since he had kissed her senseless in the park.

Maggie grimaced as she recalled her futile efforts to be rid of him. Nothing, absolutely *nothing* discouraged the man—not frosty looks, not curt, monosyllabic replies, not stony silence. Clint merely chuckled and paced his steps to hers.

While she jogged along in tight-lipped silence, he carried on a one-sided conversation, telling her about his childhood, his family, his hopes for the future.

In the last three weeks she'd learned all about his mother and his two brothers and their families. She had come to recognize the affectionate tone he employed when talking about his mother, the unmistakable warmth and love in his voice when he spoke of his dead wife. And in spite of all her self-chastisement, Maggie *was* intrigued.

It was over a week before she had realized that she was being wooed with a subtle blend of tenderness and teasing, which she had to admit she found darned near irresistible. Only by constantly reminding herself that the man was about as faithful as a roving tomcat did she manage to hold on to her protective facade of frosty indifference.

But even when her defenses cracked under his potent

male charm, as they did every now and then, they were quickly shored up by his daily, abrasive phone calls. Somehow he managed to find something wrong with every show. How, she wondered, could he possibly imagine that they could have any sort of personal relationship when he jumped down her throat with hobnailed boots every afternoon?

Moaning, Maggie thrust the fingers of both hands through her silky hair and pressed her palms tightly against the sides of her head. The man's method of separating his personal and professional lives was driving her around the bend! Between his constant badgering and his relentless pursuit he had her so confused she was tied up in knots.

She knew, of course, that she could avoid the early morning encounters by simply jogging elsewhere, but that smacked of running away, which to Maggie was the same as admitting defeat, and that was out of the question. Clint Rafferty had managed to challenge her on both a personal and a professional level, a situation her basic nature would not allow her to ignore or evade. And she had a sneaking suspicion he knew it.

Angry with herself for once again letting her thoughts stray to Clint, Maggie marched back to her desk and snatched up the production report. "You've got more important things to do than fret over that great, hulking Don Juan," she scolded, dropping down into her chair and fixing her eyes determinedly on the column of figures.

For the rest of the day Maggie applied herself to her job like a small dervish, checking background material and dictating letters to prospective guests, setting up the taping schedule, briefing Alex on the guest for the next show, reviewing with Marvin Ketchum, the show's director, and the crew of technicians, the pretaped segments scheduled for use the following week. Late in the day she even managed to collar J.D. long enough to present her case for increasing the show's budget. Then, on returning to her own office, she had to listen to ten minutes of complaints from the wardrobe mistress.

Immersed in the myriad of problems and details inherent in producing a daily TV show, Maggie was able to push aside her personal problems while at the station, but at home that escape was not available.

All weekend she paced and fidgeted and worried incessantly over the outcome of the survey. And to make matters worse, it seemed to her that Clint was intensifying his efforts. During their early morning runs on Saturday and Sunday he was charming and amusing and utterly beguiling, making it even harder than usual to refuse when he asked her out, as he did daily. By the end of the weekend Maggie reluctantly faced the fact that the man was slowly wearing down her resistance, and the admission did nothing at all to relieve her anxiety.

On Monday morning she arrived at the station for her meeting with Henry and Clint in a state of high tension, only to find that the results of the survey were disappointingly inconclusive.

Though respectable, the gain in their adult audience was not as impressive as Maggie had hoped. Luckily, however, the fact that a large percentage of the viewers, from all backgrounds, approved of the show's format and professed to shop regularly at Sporting Chance was enough to convince Henry that the trial period should be extended.

"I think we should give it another month. Let the viewers adjust to the new time," he declared magnanimously, his beaming smile bouncing back and forth between J.D. and Maggie.

Not daring to breathe, she looked quickly at Clint,

who lounged back in a leather chair on the other side of J.D.'s desk. He was watching her thoughtfully over steepled fingers, his eyes narrowed and calculating.

Maggie tensed, sure he was going to object to Henry's suggestion, but finally he gave a resigned shrug and muttered grudgingly, "Okay. You've got one more month. But I'm warning you, Maggie, the next survey had better be more impressive than this one or else"— he paused, his eyes sparkling with a sly, wicked glint— "I'm afraid you'll have to develop a taste for a certain black bird."

Smiling pleasantly, her eyes like blue chips of ice, Maggie rose to her feet. "Well, since I've never developed a taste for fowl of any kind and have no intention of doing so now, I guess I'd better get cracking, hadn't I." After bestowing a polite smile on the other two men, she excused herself and sauntered out of the room with all the confidence of a riverboat gambler in a room full of country bumpkins.

Determined not to be the one to eat crow, Maggie worked flat out over the next few weeks, stretching both herself and the show's budget to the outer limits. She even managed to pressure J.D. into letting her produce a thirty-second promo for the show, which was aired daily at regular intervals.

Though "Houston Today" continued to focus on cultural and educational subjects, Maggie made a concerted effort to book guests that would appeal to the rugged sportsman or athlete. Over the next few weeks their lineup included a team of mountain climbers, a race car driver, a top-seeded tennis player, a professional rodeo cowboy, and an official of the American Olympics Committee. One entire show was even given over to a debate between the proponents of gun control and the members of a local sportsman's club. If "Houston Today" failed to grab the lion's share of the sports-oriented viewers, Maggie was determined it wouldn't be from lack of trying.

"Now, I ask you, did you ever see two sexier hunks?" breathed one of the women hovering in the shadows surrounding the set, her eyes fixed on Alex and his guest. "It ought to be against the law for those two to be on the same show together. All that raw sex appeal is enough to drive the women in the audience berserk."

"I'll say," her companion groaned in agreement. "My libido went into overdrive the minute I saw them. It's all I can do right now to keep from running onto the set tearing my clothes off."

"Personally, I'd rather tear their clothes off," the first woman purred.

Standing a few feet away, Maggie fought back a grin as she listened to the breathless conversation. Slowly, she let her eyes scan the studio, and a knowing smile tilted her lips upward. It was amazing how many of the female staff at Channel 6 had suddenly found an urgent reason to visit the set.

Not that Maggie could really blame them. Nick Lawson was one of the most attractive young men she'd ever seen, and seated next to Alex, the two of them were a breathtaking study in masculine beauty and appeal. Both blond and handsome, Alex was the epitome of the smooth, polished sophisticate, while Nick, with his casual, devil-may-care rakishness, was the rugged individualist. It was no wonder all the feminine hearts in the building were atwitter.

Marv Ketchum gave the wrap-up signal, and Maggie watched in admiration as Alex deftly brought the show to a close. A moment later, when the set lights went out and the picture faded from the monitor, she stepped forward.

"That was great. Thank you, Nick, for coming," she said, extending her hand to Alex's guest. "I know with your busy schedule this was probably an imposition, but we do appreciate it."

"Think nothing of it, Maggie," Nick Lawson drawled. He took her hand and held it between both of his. His eyes crinkled attractively as he smiled down at her. "I was glad to do it, believe me. Particularly since it gave me an excuse to see you again."

Maggie laughed and disengaged her hand, dismissing his flirtatious comment without so much as a flutter. "Well, whatever the reason, we're grateful. And if I don't see you again while you're in town, good luck on your picture. I hope it's a smash." She smiled a quick farewell then caught Alex's eye. "Drop by my office before you go, will you, Alex? I want to brief you on a slight change in Friday's lineup."

"Sure thing, Maggie," Alex agreed readily.

Sending Nick one last smile, she turned away. She was almost to her office before he caught up with her.

"Maggie, could I see you for a moment?"

She turned, surprised to see him striding after her. "Yes, of course," she said as he came to a halt in front of her.

Now that he had her attention Nick seemed strangely hesitant. He stood with thumbs hooked in the back pockets of his jeans, his expression unsure. A rueful smile twisting one corner of his mouth as he stared down into her expectant face. "Well, the thing is . . . I was wondering if you'd have dinner with me tonight?" he asked finally.

Surprise widened Maggie's eyes. She certainly hadn't been expecting that. Nick Lawson was twenty-eight, five years her junior. It had never occurred to her that he might want to see her socially. Especially when he could have his pick of just about any woman in town.

Sensing her hesitation, Nick urged quickly, "Please say yes, Maggie. I'd like very much to get to know you better. I wanted to the last time I was here, but Alex told me then that you had just gotten a divorce and weren't dating anyone yet, so I didn't push."

Feeling immensely flattered and not a little embarrassed, Maggie bit her lip in confusion. She liked Nick very much, but she was too old for him. Or he was too young for her, one of the two. She couldn't possibly go out with him. But even as she opened her mouth to tell him, there suddenly flashed through her mind a picture of Clint and his young, nubile girlfriends, and she thought—why not?

The strange defiant mood that prompted Maggie to accept Nick's invitation stayed with her for the rest of the day. At eight that night, wearing the sexiest little black dress she owned, she sailed out the front door on Nick's arm, determined to have a good time if it killed her.

"Do you·think they'll recover?" Nick asked as they reached the plush Mercedes at the curb.

"Maybe in about a week," Maggie whispered, glancing back over her shoulder at the gaping teenagers framed in the open doorway.

Because of a school holiday the next day Allison was once again spending the night with Laura. Both girls had hovered over her as she dressed for the evening, trying, none to subtly, to find out who her date was. Maggie hadn't told them. She thought it would be much more fun to surprise them, since they were both Nick Lawson fans. It had not only been fun . . . it had been hilarious. The moment Nick walked in Laura's and

Allison's mouths had dropped open, exactly as though someone had slipped the hinge pins out of their jaws. All through the introduction both had simply gaped, mute as two fence posts.

"Good. I'd hate to see them go through life that way. They'll catch flies."

Much to Maggie's surprise, she had a marvelous time. Nick proved to be every bit as nice as she had thought he would be, and as the evening wore on she liked him more and more. They enjoyed a pleasant meal at a small but exclusive restaurant and afterward danced and talked for hours. He was a charming, interesting, very attentive escort, and for a while Maggie was able to put Clint out of her mind. Almost.

It was close to one in the morning when Nick walked Maggie to her front door. She was feeling relaxed and happy, and when he drew her into his arms she didn't resist.

His kiss was pleasant and warm, and Maggie returned it willingly. It was nice, Maggie decided, to be kissed, to be desired by this young man. Nice—but not earthshaking. And certainly not threatening. When Nick parted her lips and his tongue sought hers in a tentative caress, Maggie sighed and relaxed against him.

"It's about time you got home. Where the hell have you been?"

The deep, angry voice cracked over them like a whip. Startled, Maggie tore herself out of Nick's arms and whirled to face the man silhouetted in the open doorway, her eyes growing huge.

"Clint! What are you doing here?"

He was a menacing figure, standing with his legs braced apart, hands on his hips, glaring at the younger man as though he'd like nothing better than to punch him. "I'm here because our daughters called me," he barked. "They heard a noise and were scared. I promised them I'd stay until you came home." His lips curled in disgust as his gaze sliced back and forth between Maggie and Nick. "I was beginning to think you weren't going to."

Maggie stiffened. "Of course I was coming home!" she snapped. Why was it that he could make her feel like a teenager who'd been caught necking in the back seat of a car?

She turned and gave Nick an apologetic look. "Nick, this is Allison's father, Clinton Rafferty." Her frosty gaze darted to the other man. "Clint, meet Nick Lawson."

The two men eyed one another warily, exchanging only the barest of nods. The air on the porch fairly bristled with male hostility and aggression.

"Look, Nick, I'm sorry our evening had to end this way," Maggie said into the awkward silence, placing her hand on his arm. "But I had a lovely time. Really."

"That's all right, Maggie. No harm done." Nick's gaze collided once again with Clint's, and when he looked back at Maggie there was a determined gleam in his eye. Bending over, he brushed a kiss across her lips, then smiled. "I'll call you," he whispered huskily, and with a curt nod at the other man, he turned and walked away.

When his car had disappeared around the corner Maggie gave Clint a murderous glare, then brushed past him and stalked into the house. She was stepping out of her shoes, just inside the foyer, when he slammed the door with a resounding bang.

Tiny came bounding down the stairs woofing a greeting, but a sharp command from Clint sent him scurrying back up. Maggie took exception to his high-handed manner, but before she could say a word he advanced on her like some avenging angel and thundered, "Just what in hell do you think you're doing, going out with that young stud?"

For just an instant Maggie's jaw dropped, but it was quickly snapped shut. *"What?"* She thrust out her chin and planted her balled fists on her hips. "Now see here. My personal life comes under the heading of none of your damned business!"

"When the girls have to call on me for help because you're too busy running around with a kid young enough to be—"

"So help me, Rafferty, if you say 'my son' I'm going to punch you right in the mouth!" Maggie flared indignantly. "For your information there is only five years' difference in our ages!"

"Five!" Clint drew an exasperated breath and looked up at the ceiling. "Good grief, Maggie. I never thought you'd stoop to cradle robbing."

"Cra—!" Maggie made a strangled sound in the back of her throat and rolled her eyes in supplication. "I don't believe this! I simply don't believe it! *I'm* being lectured on this subject by *you?* That's a laugh! Talk about the pot calling the kettle black!"

"Dammit, he's too young for you!" Clint roared.

Maggie was so angry that for a moment she couldn't even speak. She glared at Clint, her small body quivering with fury. When she found her voice it vibrated with suppressed feeling. "I don't have to take this. Especially not from a man whose latest girlfriend still wears a retainer to bed," she snapped, whirling on one stocking-clad foot and stomping into the living room. Clint was right behind her.

"Would you mind explaining to me why, after weeks of knocking myself out, I've gotten exactly nowhere with you, yet the minute that Hollywood rooster struts into town you go out with him?''

She turned on him, her spine stiff, her fists parked aggressively on her hipbones. Clint towered over her like a mountain, but she wasn't in the least intimidated by his size. "No, I will not! I don't have to explain my actions to you. It's my life, and if I want to . . . aaugh!''

Maggie's breath left her lungs in a loud whoosh as Clint grabbed her shoulders and hauled her up against his chest. "Ah, sweet heaven, Maggie, you're driving me crazy!'' Cupping a hand beneath her chin, Clint tilted her head back at a sharp angle and bent to find her mouth with his.

It wasn't fair! It simply wasn't fair, Maggie railed silently as she felt her body's immediate response. Her heart was kicking against her ribs as though it were trying to escape, and there was a fiery sensation racing through her veins. Her knees turned to rubber. She felt hot and cold all over.

That she had felt drawn to him, even when he was yelling at her, had merely added to her fury, but the moment he had touched her her anger had been reduced to ashes. Her mind might resist him, but her body had other ideas, ideas that had nothing whatever to do with common sense or intelligent choices. She was flooded with sensations, aching with need. It wasn't fair, she repeated feebly to herself one last time before giving in with a fatalistic little moan to the demands that had become irresistible.

She melted against him and opened her mouth to his demanding kiss. Clint groaned and stabbed his tongue into the sweet warmth, plundering her mouth with a possessive tenderness that made her heart stop for an instant, then take off at an even more thunderous rate.

His lips were warm, his tongue warmer, and he

tasted of coffee and whiskey and male. The kiss grew deeper, better, and Maggie felt the sensual pleasure of it all the way to her toes. Her hands slid up over the hard planes of his chest to curve around his neck, her fingers threading through the cool strands of raven-black hair as she strained to move closer.

With a groan, Clint stooped, curved an arm beneath her bottom, and lifted her high against his chest. Holding her clamped to him, his mouth still fused with hers, he moved to the couch and in a single fluid motion stretched out on his back with Maggie draped on top of him. A soft moan of pleasure escaped Maggie as her soft form pressed against his aroused body.

Clint released her from his enveloping embrace, and his large hands roamed over her back, her hips, the backs of her thighs. His body shifted restlessly beneath her slight weight.

Their new position gave Maggie a heady feeling of power, and her mouth played with his, nipping and tasting, sucking gently. She held his head between her hands and very slowly, with a teasing, feathery touch, explored the swirls of his ears and the sides of his neck. When he shuddered beneath her she trailed her finger-tips down over his jaw, enjoying the slight rasp of his beard stubble against her sensitive skin.

When Clint tried to deepen the kiss once again, Maggie pulled her mouth from his to string a line of stinging little love bites across his face.

"Oh, God, Maggie! Yes . . . yes." His hands clutched her bottom, the long fingers gripping fiercely as he pressed her into even greater intimacy.

Maggie moaned, then gasped as he bent his head and kissed her breast through the silky material of her dress. Clint's mouth caressed her until Maggie thought she would faint.

"Sweet . . . so sweet," Clint groaned. "Oh, Maggie. You're so tiny . . . but you're all woman. Too much woman for that young boy. I can satisfy you so much better than he ever could, darling."

As he spoke he shifted to roll Maggie beneath him but before her back had touched the sofa his words penetrated her brain like icy shards.

Self-disgust and anger flooded through her in a tidal wave. She jerked out of Clint's embrace and rolled to the floor, then shot up and began to back away, her face mirroring her anguish.

Caught completely off guard, it took Clint a moment to react. He looked at her blankly, then lifted up on his elbows. His brows met over his nose in a confused frown. "What's wrong?"

"Everything's wrong," Maggie blurted out, gesturing wildly with one hand. "You. Me. This whole thing."

The thread of panic in her voice brought a softening smile to Clint's face. His eyes were tender and inviting as he shook his head and held out his hand. "No it isn't, sweetheart. Come back here and I'll show you just how right everything is." His voice dropped to just above a whisper. "Come let me love you, Maggie."

"No!" She backed away another step. "No, I can't. It was all a mistake. I . . . you . . . I, uh, didn't mean for this to happen. Things . . . things just got out of hand. I'm sorry."

Clint sprang up off the sofa and started for her, smiling gently. "It wasn't a mistake, love. Far from it. We're attracted to each other, Maggie. This has been inevitable since we first met." Maggie's anger began to rise and her face tightened, but Clint went on as though he hadn't noticed. "We're going to be good together, Maggie. Come here. Let me show you."

He reached for her, but Maggie slapped his hand away and took another step backward, glowering blackly. "I said no," she snapped. "You've got a lot of nerve, calling Nick a stud, when you have a whole string of young, sexy females at your beck and call. Well, if you think for one moment I have any intention of becoming the old gray mare in your stable of young fillies, you've got mush for brains."

Clint halted, his face growing hard as he read the determination in hers. He lifted his head proudly and stared at her through narrowed green eyes. "That was a cheap shot, Maggie."

"Maybe so. But I think I got my point across."

"Oh, yes. You certainly did that."

Refusing to be swayed by the hurt look in his eyes, Maggie lifted her chin and said haughtily. "I think you'd better leave now."

Clint turned and stalked out of the living room. At the door he stopped and turned. "You may rest assured, Mrs. Trent, that I won't bother you again."

Maggie winced as the door slammed behind him. Slowly, dejectedly, she sat down in the winged-backed chair and curled her bare feet beneath her. She swallowed hard against the painful tightness in her throat and told herself it was for the best. "After all, it's not as though I'm in love with the man," she murmured shakily.

Upstairs, two silent figures, huddled on the landing, looked down into the empty foyer and shook their heads sadly.

"Adults!" Allison muttered in disgust. "It's really amazing how blockheaded they can be sometimes."

"Yeah," Laura agreed on a disconsolate sigh. "And for a minute there everything seemed to be working out just like we planned. I wonder what your dad said to set Mom off like that?"

"Something really dumb, no doubt.

"So what do we do now?"

"I don't know yet. It'd serve them right if we just gave up on them." Allison sighed heavily. "But we won't. Eventually they've got to come to their senses."

Chapter Six

Agitated and unhappy, and not quite sure why, Maggie spent the next two hours pacing the floor. She was so exhausted by the time she finally did crawl into bed that she forgot to set the alarm and overslept the next morning. For the first time in years she was forced to skip her morning jog. As it was she barely had time to shower and throw herself into a dark gold wool dress and step into a pair of brown lizard pumps. Sprinting out the back door, her purse slung over her shoulder and car keys clamped between her teeth, she fumbled with one hand to fasten the buckle on her belt while wielding a hairbrush with the other.

When Maggie rushed into her office twenty minutes later, her phone was ringing. Simultaneously, she kicked off her shoes, dumped her purse into a drawer, and picked up the receiver.

"Maggie Trent," she panted into the mouthpiece, groping behind her for her chair.

"Where the hell were you this morning?"

Maggie sat down abruptly. "What?"

"Where were you?" Clint repeated forcefully, his voice carrying the sting of a whip. "I waited around in that damned park for over an hour. Then I got worried that maybe something had happened to you on the way, but when I called the girls they said you had already left for work. What did you do, jog somewhere else because you didn't want to face me? Well hear this, little Maggie, we may never be lovers but I'm not about to abandon you to the park perverts. If I have to I'll wait for you on your doorstep every morning. In fact, that's not a bad idea."

Maggie went from puzzlement to surprise to sheer vexation in the space of a few seconds. "Will you please let me get a word in edgewise," she ground out tightly. "I didn't jog elsewhere. I simply didn't jog. And not because I was trying to avoid you. I overslept this morning and didn't have time."

"Why? Are you ill?"

His quick switch from anger to concern threw Maggie for a moment. She bit her lower lip as she felt the resentment draining out of her. Drat the man! He had no right to do this to her! She didn't want his tenderness! "No, I'm not ill. I just forgot to set the alarm. That's all."

There was a long pause. That was not all, and they both knew it. After a moment Clint said, "I see. Well, in that case, I'll see you in the morning."

And she did. The next morning and every morning after that he was waiting for her at the end of the drive when she stepped out of the house. Side by side, while Tiny cavorted around them in joyous abandon, they covered the few short blocks to the park, ran the usual number of laps, then returned to Maggie's home, with hardly a word spoken between them. When they did talk their conversations were stiff and formal, consisting mostly of perfunctory hellos and goodbyes, with a few desultory comments on the weather or something equally innocuous thrown in. Beneath the surface there was an undercurrent of anger and wariness running between them which neither made any attempt to allay.

During this period Maggie redoubled her efforts to ensure that the next survey would be in their favor. But as a precautionary measure, she had several meetings with the station's sales manager, alerting him to the possibility that they might need a new sponsor for "Houston Today." Just in case.

Trying to track down and sign interesting guests, Maggie spent hours on the phone and made numerous short trips out of town, often not getting home until late. Luckily for the state of her conscience, Laura was equally busy.

The school band had been picked to play in the Macy's Thanksgiving Day Parade, and for the last year the kids had washed cars, mowed lawns, and done a variety of odd jobs to raise money for the trip. Recently, during the hectic last few weeks before the holiday, they had spent every afternoon after school and most of the weekends drilling and rehearsing for the big event.

Laura and Allison could hardly wait. The entire band was going up a day early, but after the parade the girls were to spend the remainder of the long holiday weekend with Maggie's brother, Dennis, and his family in Connecticut, then fly home Sunday night. Both girls were so excited over the prospect that they nearly drove Maggie crazy with their constant chatter and giggling. She began to look forward to their departure almost as much as they did.

The night before they were to leave Maggie was

packing Laura's suitcase when her daughter trailed dejectedly into the room and plopped down on the bed, sighing dramatically. Maggie looked up and raised a quizzical brow.

"What's the long face for?"

"I just talked to Allison on the phone. She's not going to New York," Laura quavered pathetically.

Pausing in the act of folding a sweater, Maggie looked up again, her eyes wide with surprise. "Not going? Why not? The two of you have talked of nothing else for weeks."

"Her dad is sick, and she won't leave him alone with no one to look after him."

Maggie's heart gave a queer little lurch. "Sick? How is he sick? What's wrong with him?"

"He's got the three-day measles."

Maggie stared, her mouth open. "Measles?" she squeaked. "Clint has the *measles?*"

"Yeah," Laura confirmed in a tone that reeked with disgust. "And Allison says he's mad as a hornet."

Maggie couldn't help it. She clamped a hand over her mouth, but the giggle came out anyway. The thought of Clint Rafferty covered in red spots was simply too much for her. She sputtered and choked and tried hard to keep a straight face, but it was no use. There was no way she could hold her mirth in check. Ignoring her daughter's stern expression, Maggie fell back on the bed and howled.

"Oh, that's pr-priceless," she burbled between hoots of laughter. "Clinton Rafferty, super jock and . . . la-ladies' man, felled by the me- . . . me- . . . measles!" The last came out on a rising note as Maggie was once again overcome with the giggles. "Oh, I . . . lo-love it!"

"Moth-errrr!" Laura admonished with a scowl, giv-

ing the single word all the dramatic emphasis only a teenager can. "Honestly! You have the most warped sense of humor sometimes. It isn't at all funny. Allison says he feels terrible and he's running a high fever."

Guiltily squelching her laughter, Maggie struggled up on her elbows and tried her best to look apologetic. "I'm sorry, darling. You're right. I shouldn't have laughed. But, dear, a fever is common with the three-day measles, and if Mr. Rafferty will just stay in bed and take it easy for a few days he should be just fine."

"Try telling that to Allison," Laura muttered glumly. "She says she's not going to leave him all alone."

Looking at her daughter's downbent head and the dejected slump of her shoulders, Maggie felt a tug on her heartstrings. It wasn't the end of the world, of course, but to two thirteen year olds it must certainly seem like it. She sat up and slid over to Laura's side and put her arm around her. "I'm sorry, darling. I wish there was something I could do."

Laura sighed heavily. "Allison says her father is helpless when he's sick."

"Most men are," Maggie said with a chuckle.

"Of course, if she could get someone else to stay with him"—Laura paused and gave her mother a sidelong look—"someone she really trusts . . . she'd probably go."

It took a moment for Laura's meaning to sink in. When it did, Maggie's eyes grew round, and she shook her head. "No. Oh, no. Not me," she began vehemently. "The answer is definitely no. You're not going to talk me into playing nursemaid to that man."

"Oh *please,* Mom. *Please,*" Laura wailed. "I'll just *die* if Allison doesn't get to go with me. I swear I will. You've just *got* to do this for us."

"Laura, I simply ca—"

Laura grabbed her mother's hands, her brown eyes fixing her with a beseeching look guaranteed to melt stone. "Please, Mom. Say you'll do it. Unless there's a problem at the station you've got the rest of the week off, so you're free to look after him. And all you'll have to do is prepare his meals and see that he gets his rest. It won't be any trouble for you."

Oh, Laura, Maggie groaned silently, as she tried in vain to resist her daughter's appealing look. You don't know what you're saying. Sick or well, Clinton Rafferty spells trouble in capital letters.

Her expression pained, she stared back at Laura, trying to dredge up the strength to refuse and failing miserably. She simply wasn't ogre enough to deny the girls this trip, even if it meant spending five days under the same roof with Clint.

Feeling like the absolute prize sucker of all time, Maggie grimaced, rolled her eyes heavenward, and sighed. "Oh, all right. I'll do it."

Even as the words came out of her mouth she could hardly believe she'd said them.

"Ooohhh, Mom, you're terrific!" Laura squealed her delight and threw her arms around her mother's neck, then, in one continuous motion, spun around and headed for the door, calling over her shoulder, "I'll go phone Allison and tell her the good news."

A wan smile—part maternal pleasure at her daughter's happiness and part pure panic—played around the corners of Maggie's mouth. Maybe Allison won't agree, she told herself hopefully as she listened to Laura lope down the stairs two at a time. Or maybe Clint would refuse to have her.

The smile turned into a grimace. *Oh sure, Maggie, sure. And maybe J.D. will double your salary tomorrow. Fat chance! The man will probably take a fiendish*

delight in having you wait on him hand and foot.
Snatching up the remaining items of clothing, Maggie
thrust them into the suitcase with scant regard for
neatness. "You're a fool, Maggie Trent," she berated
herself as she banged the case shut and snapped the
locks. "A complete and utter fool."

She was still calling herself names the next morning
when, after seeing the girls off at the airport, she let
herself into the Rafferty home with the key Allison had
given her.

She paused in the dimly lit foyer and listened for
signs of life, but the house was as quiet as a tomb. Clint
must still be asleep, Maggie decided as she turned and
very carefully eased the door shut and flipped the lock.
Stealthily, she tiptoed across the hall and placed her
small weekend bag beside the stairs, then shucked out
of her coat and draped it across the newel post. Sitting
down on the bottom step, she unzipped her high-heeled
boots and tugged them off, pulled the thick, brightly
patterned socks back up to her knees, and adjusted the
legs of her jeans down over them. With a sigh, she
stretched her legs out in front of her and wriggled her
liberated toes. Heaven!

She stood and adjusted the ribbed hem of her
wine-red velour top down over her hips. For a moment
Maggie considered going upstairs to check on Clint,
then decided against it and padded soundlessly toward
the door at the end of the hall, which she assumed led
to the kitchen. She pushed through the swinging door
and came to an abrupt halt at the sight of the masculine
form that seemed to be attempting to crawl into the
refrigerator.

"What are you doing up?" she demanded.

Clint jumped, and the back of his head came into
sharp contact with the metal rack above it. A muffled,

but extremely colorful stream of oaths poured from the frosty depths of the refrigerator for several seconds before he extricated himself and swung to face her, rubbing the back of his head and glowering.

The navy blue terrycloth robe he was wearing was barely decent, ending at mid-thigh, and Maggie had a strong suspicion he was quite naked beneath it. His rumpled hair was sticking up at all angles. His face was puffy and blotched with red bumps, which spread down over his neck and chest and disappeared beneath the forest of dark hairs at the opening of his carelessly tied robe. Even his hard-muscled, hairy legs were mottled a rosy color, all the way down to his bare feet. Maggie's mouth went dry. Spotted or not, the sight of his near naked body did disturbing things to her insides.

"What are you doing here?"

Maggie blinked, taken aback for a moment. "I'm here to take care of you while the girls are gone, like we arranged."

"Arranged, hell! I told Allison I didn't need anyone to nursemaid me. Especially not you. So you can just put your shoes back on and haul that cute little tush right out of here."

Maggie's tush didn't move. If he had tried all week, Clint couldn't have said anything more guaranteed to make her bow her neck and dig in her heels. *So he doesn't want me. Well, too bad.* Completely ignoring the fact that only minutes before she would have been overjoyed to hear that she didn't have to spend the weekend with this man, she tilted her chin and glowered right back.

"I'll ask you one more time. What are you doing out of bed?"

"I was trying to eat breakfast, before *you* barged in."

For the first time Maggie noticed that Clint held a can

of beer in one hand and that there was a plate containing a wedge of extremely old-looking chocolate pie sitting on the kitchen table. Her gaze slid from the pie to the beer can, then back, her face taking on a sickly cast as a nauseating suspicion began to form in her mind. "Don't tell me that's breakfast," she questioned in an appalled tone.

"Yes, that's breakfast," Clint grated, popping the top off the beer and slamming it down beside the pie. "I'm hungry, I'm thirsty, my throat feels like I swallowed a wad of cotton, and I'm running a fever. Surely you don't expect me to stand over a stove and cook bacon and eggs?"

"Certainly not!" Maggie snapped testily. "That's what I'm here for."

"Hey! What are you doing?" Clint yelped when she marched over to the table and snatched up his disgusting excuse for a breakfast.

Ignoring his outraged sputtering, Maggie turned, dumped the crusted pie into the disposal side of the sink, and poured the beer over it. The foaming liquid broke the brown glob into wet clumps, and as the combined smells of chocolate and beer rose from the sink, Maggie's stomach flip-flopped.

"Now," she said calmly. "If you'll go back to bed like a good boy, I'll prepare a decent breakfast and bring it to you."

Clint's red-blotched skin turned even redder. For a minute he looked as though the top of his head was about to blow off. But instead of cowering under his blistering rage, Maggie faced him squarely, pointed an imperious finger toward the door, and using her most commanding tone, clipped, "Bed. Right now."

There wasn't a doubt in Maggie's mind that Clint was itching to strangle her, but she stood her ground, her stern gaze locked with his. For a full ten seconds Clint fought a silent battle within himself, then swallowed his rage and stomped toward the door.

"I'll go to bed all right. But only because I feel too damned bad to stand here and argue with you. However, I expect you to be out of here by the time I reach the top of the stairs. Is that clear?"

Maggie smirked at the violently swinging kitchen door for a moment before calmly opening the refrigerator and bending to inspect its contents.

Clint's bedroom door was ajar when she climbed the stairs half an hour later. Carefully balancing the loaded tray, she nudged it open with her hip and stepped inside. She met his frowning look with complete serenity.

"I thought you'd be gone by now," he growled, but Maggie noticed he was eyeing the tray with interest.

Struggling into a sitting position, Clint sent her a dark look. The bunched covers slid immodestly around his narrow hips, stopping just short of indecent exposure.

The tray rattled in Maggie's hands as she tried not to notice the impossibly broad shoulders and brawny chest tapering down to a board-flat abdomen. But she found the inverted triangle of dark hair utterly fascinating and swallowed hard as her eyes followed its narrowing path to where it whorled enticingly around his navel before continuing downward to disappear beneath the edge of the rumpled sheet. The thin covers molded his body with heart-stopping accuracy. Her heart began to pound wildly. Finally, realizing she was staring, Maggie jerked her head up.

"If you have a fever you should cover up," she snapped waspishly, while her eyes telegraphed another message: *Just one wisecrack out of you, Rafferty, and I'll upend this tray in your lap.*

But either Clint possessed a prudent sense of self-preservation or he was still too angry to notice her intimate perusal. He gave her an exasperated look and frantically scratched his chest and arms with both hands. "I itch too much to cover up," he snarled. "And I thought I told you to leave."

Unperturbed, Maggie plopped the tray down on his thighs. "I promised Allison I'd take care of you, and that's what I'm going to do, so quit arguing." Grabbing up the box she had placed on the tray along with his breakfast, she turned and headed for the bathroom.

"Where are you going?"

"To run your bath."

"I've already showered this morning," he informed her indignantly.

"This is not for getting clean, you idiot, it's for what ails you." She waggled the box at him. "This is baking soda. Dissolved in warm water, it's excellent for relieving itching. After you've soaked for about twenty minutes I'll rub you down with calamine lotion. You'll be surprised at how much better you'll feel."

At the mention of a rubdown Clint brightened visibly and, without another word of protest, picked up his fork and attacked the steaming poached eggs on his plate.

Maggie emerged from the bathroom just as he was wolfing down the last of his breakfast, and she gestured toward the door. "Your bath is ready. While you soak I'll change the sheets."

"Oh, all right," Clint grumbled, setting the tray on the bedside table.

Maggie expected him to put on the robe that was lying across the foot of the bed. Instead he calmly flipped back the covers, stood up and started for the bathroom . . . naked as the day he was born.

Maggie gasped and averted her eyes. To her annoyance, she felt herself blush all the way down to her toes. Her ears burned as though they were on fire.

Frantically, she turned and jerked open a dresser drawer and began to paw through it.

"What are you looking for?"

"Pajamas. Surely you have some."

"Nope. Never use 'em."

"You mean you sleep like that with a thirteen-year-old daughter in the house?" Maggie demanded, scandalized.

"Certainly. Allison knows better than to barge in without knocking."

Maggie slammed the drawer shut, marched over to the bed, and began ripping off the blankets and sheets, carefully keeping her eyes away from Clint. *It was certainly going to be a long five days.*

Pausing in the bathroom doorway, Clint watched her agitated movements and shook his head in disgust. "For Pete's sake! What are you so het up about? You've seen a man before. You've been married."

Still presenting him with her stiff back, Maggie picked up a pillow and peeled off the wrinkled pillowcase. "Not to you, thank God!" she snapped.

There was a thick pause, followed by a furiously clipped, "You got that right. No man in his right mind would want to be married to a little icicle like you."

Before she could reply, the bathroom door slammed shut.

Maggie whirled around and glared at the door as though she could incinerate it with her eyes. She knew he had meant for the remark to rile her, and it had. But *if you think I'm going to be tricked into proving you're wrong, think again,* she vowed silently.

When Clint emerged from the bathroom, she was waiting for him. Very coolly, she appraised him from head to toe, gave a dismissive little shrug and gestured toward the bed. "Lie down on your stomach and I'll apply this lotion to your spots."

One black brow shot upward at her bored tone, but after a brief pause Clint complied, stretching out in the middle of the king-size bed. Maggie clambered across the mattress on her knees and sat back on her feet beside him. A tiny smile of fiendish anticipation curled the corners of her mouth upward. After giving it a brisk shaking, she uncapped the bottle and very deliberately drizzled a thin line of the cool, pink liquid into the shallow trench that marked his spine.

Clint flinched and sucked in his breath. "Aa-ah! Couldn't you have warmed it in your palm first?"

"Sorry," Maggie chirped with a complete lack of sympathy.

With slow, silken strokes she began to spread the lotion over his shoulders and down his arms all the way to his wrist, threading her fingers through the curling black hairs on his forearms, coating them with the fast-drying pink stuff. Wet fingertips slid delicately across his neck and around his ears, then became bolder as they kneaded the broad expanse of muscled flesh across his back.

Periodically, she dolloped more lotion on him and spread it ever lower, in a sensuous, circular motion. When her hands dipped below his waist she felt a tremor quake through Clint's body, the muscles beneath the warm bronze flesh quivering. Growing bolder, Maggie straddled his legs and drizzled more lotion over the base of his spine. She smeared her hands through it and gripped the firm buttocks with spread fingers, letting her wet palms slip and slide over the tight mounds of flesh. Erotically, one lotion-coated fingertip on each hand slowly traced the underside of his buttocks where they curved into the back of his thighs.

Clint groaned and buried his face on his crossed arms.

A trembling excitement she couldn't control was building within Maggie at the delicious feel of muscle and bone and warm flesh beneath her sensitive palms. The symmetry of Clint's magnificent body, with all its powerful grace, held her mesmerized. Her heart was pounding with a slow, heavy beat, and she could barely breathe. Her throat was dry. Every tremor that shook Clint's body produced an answering one in hers.

Maggie knew she should stop, but somehow her hands just kept stroking and gliding over him as though they had a will of their own. And the further she went, the more she experienced the exquisite tactile pleasure of touching him, the more impossible it was to stop. She watched in helpless fascination as her long, slender fingers smoothed the lotion over his strong thighs, the backs of his knees, and the bunched muscles of his calves, the feathery touch of his hair-roughened skin against her palms sending tiny shock waves up her arms and raising gooseflesh all over her. By the time she reached his feet, she was weak with desire, barely able to breathe.

"Are you finished?" Clint's voice was a raspy whisper that made her feel hot, then cold, then hot again.

"Ye-yes," Maggie stammered hoarsely, and her heart took a giant leap up into her throat when Clint began, very slowly, to turn over onto his back.

His eyes burned into her like emerald fires. His face was taut and flushed with desire, tinting the measle blotches a deep shade of crimson. There was no way he could hide his arousal . . . and no way Maggie could ignore it.

He reached out his hand to her, inviting her to come closer. Maggie knelt uncertainly at his feet, her mouth quivering. His voice thick with passion, eyes entreating, Clint murmured, "You've cured one itch, sweetheart, but you've created another one. One only you can ease." A seductive smile played about his lips, and his voice dropped to a velvet whisper. "Come scratch me, Maggie."

Temptation pulled at Maggie like a strong undertow. Her chest was so tight it ached. She wanted to go to him. Wanted it, at that moment, more than anything else in the world. But in the back of her mind an insidious little voice kept whispering, "Remember Larry. Remember Larry."

She felt herself leaning forward, felt herself reaching out to Clint, and suddenly panic overwhelmed her. With jerky motions, she capped the bottle of lotion and slapped it into his outstretched palm.

"Here, you can do your front," she blurted out in a strangled voice as she scrambled off the bed and made a dash for the door.

Maggie didn't even slow down until she reached the dubious sanctuary of the kitchen. Breathing hard, her heart drumming in her ears, she burst through the swinging door and went to stand at the sink, clutching the edge of the counter while she struggled to bring her rioting senses under control.

How did she get into these messes? She closed her eyes and shook her head. Between her outrageous sense of humor and her temper she seemed to go from one disaster to another. At least . . . she had since meeting Clint.

And she knew why. She was attracted to him, not just physically but emotionally as well. More than she had ever been attracted to any man. More than she had been attracted to her own husband, even in the beginning. And it was that emotional attraction that scared her witless.

Were it only a purely physical thing she could handle it. Out of choice she had lived a celibate existence since her divorce. It had been a period of readjustment, of assessment, a time to let her wounds heal. But she was realistic enough to know that the time would come when she would want a man in her life.

The trouble was, she would want him permanently. Despite the failure of her marriage, Maggie still held the old values. She wanted a home, a husband, a family, the closeness that comes with commitment. She wanted love. She couldn't treat sex casually, as the mere appeasement of an appetite, like many people did. In any case, she invested too much of herself in a close relationship, and she wasn't about to squander her affections on a meaningless affair.

But the better she knew Clint, the harder it was to resist him, and she had learned a lot about him during the past weeks. A lot more than she wanted to know. She knew, for instance, that when he had started making big money in pro football he had paid for his younger brothers' college educations and had built his mother a lovely home. He was generous, intelligent, and articulate. He was also gentle and caring and, when it suited him, utterly charming. As if that weren't enough, both his sense of humor and his temper were on a par with hers. In short, he was everything she had ever wanted in a man. Except faithful.

Maggie pressed her lips together and fought to suppress the weepy feeling welling up inside her. No matter what her heart told her, she couldn't let herself get involved with Clint. She was thirty-three, not eighteen. She would not be led into disaster by her emotions a second time.

For half an hour she paced around and around the

kitchen, wondering how in the world she was going to face Clint again. Finally, deciding the best way to take nasty medicine was quickly, Maggie squared her shoulders and started for the stairs.

Outside Clint's door she paused and listened, but there was no sound coming from his room. She tapped softly and waited. When there was no answer she tapped again. Still nothing. Easing the door open, she stepped inside and walked to the bed.

Clint was sound asleep.

Chapter Seven

Maggie quickly decided that as a patient, on a scale from one to ten, Clint was a zero. At the very most a one. The man accepted illness with all the grace of a bear with his foot caught in a steel trap.

She spent hours washing, peeling, and chopping vegetables for homemade soup. He picked them all out and ate only the beef and broth. When he began to itch again she repeated the soda bath and calamine treatment, this time swabbing him down with a lotion-soaked wad of cotton. He complained of the smell, the coldness, and the mess and insisted that she change the sheets again. When his fever climbed to over one hundred and one, she brought him aspirin and a flannel shirt. He refused both.

"And to think I actually went all weak and warm when I found him asleep," Maggie fumed as she sat at the kitchen table scribbling out a grocery list. Like an idiotic, lovesick fool, she had stood there gazing at him for a full five minutes, thinking how appealing and vulnerable he looked with his face relaxed in slumber, his blotchy, tanned skin coated with the powdery pink residue. Ha! How wrong could you get? The man was grumpy, argumentative, and totally uncooperative. And those were his good points!

Admittedly, her embarrassment had eased somewhat when she found him asleep. After all, if he could just calmly anoint the front of his body with lotion then roll over and take a nap, he couldn't have been all that aroused. And his behavior, since awakening, only confirmed it. He had kept her so busy she had barely had time to breathe. After running upstairs five times in less than an hour in response to his bellowed commands, Maggie decided she had to get out of the house for a while . . . before she strangled him.

"Where are you going?" Clint demanded when she walked into his room wearing her hip-length camel suede coat.

"I'm going to the supermarket first," she replied crisply, pulling on a pair of knitted, leather-palmed driving gloves. She deliberately avoided looking at Clint. "Your cupboard is almost bare, and in case you've forgotten, tomorrow is Thanksgiving. Also, I've got to stop by my house and feed Tiny."

"Good grief, Maggie! Bring the dog back with you. You can't go dashing over there every night just to feed him. Besides, he needs companionship."

"You don't mind having him here?"

"Of course not. What do you think I am, some kind of monster?"

Maggie didn't bother to answer that, but the dry look she gave him was eloquent, and Clint had the grace to flush guiltily.

"Maggie?"

She had started for the door, but the hesitancy in

Clint's voice made her turn back, and her eyes widened in surprise when she spied his contrite, almost pleading expression.

"Maggie, I know I've been a perfect pain in the neck today, and I'm sorry," he said with soft sincerity. "It's just that I've felt so rotten, and this whole thing is so embarrassing. I mean, who the hell ever heard of a grown man having the measles? It's humiliating!"

The look of disgust that contorted his features was almost too much for Maggie, and she bit the insides of her cheeks to keep from smiling. She wasn't ready to forgive him yet, but even as she watched, even as she fought to hold on to it, she felt her anger and resentment begin to drain away.

His big, capable hands were plucking absently at the covers, tugging the red wool blanket into a cluster of tiny pyramids across his chest and abdomen. His chin was tucked against his chest, and every so often he cast her a woebegone look from beneath a pathetically furrowed brow.

Damn you, Clint Rafferty, Maggie railed silently, her feelings a mixture of anger, amusement, and womanly compassion. How dare you lie there and give me that Huck Finn, repentant naughty boy look, you wretched, ungrateful beast!

But it was no use. She couldn't stay mad at a man who looked at her with such soulful, imploring eyes. Especially when what she really wanted to do was crawl into that bed and make love to him until the world spun off its axis.

"All right. Apology accepted," she said gruffly to cover her traitorous reaction. "But if I hear one more bellow from up here it will be bread and water for you for the duration."

"Yes, ma'am. I'll be good. I promise."

The unholy glint in Clint's eyes totally belied the

exaggerated solemnity of his expression. His penitence was about as genuine as a dime store emerald, and Maggie knew it. Yet, when the ghost of a smile that hovered around his mouth slowly turned into a full-fledged, devilish grin, she was helpless to stop her own lips from turning upward in response.

Ruefully shaking her head, Maggie started for the door. Clinton Rafferty was a beguiling creature when he turned on that Irish charm, and Maggie had the uneasy feeling that staying angry with him for very long would prove a Herculean task.

When she returned with Tiny an hour later, the dog immediately caught Clint's scent and began a frantic search of the house while Maggie started putting away the groceries.

"Damn you, Tiny! Get off me, you lummox!"

Maggie placed the last of the eggs in the refrigerator and paused to listen to the commotion from upstairs. Not even Clint's roared curses could stem the joyous barks of greeting. Since Clint had started jogging with Maggie every morning, Tiny's liking for the man had developed into outright adoration. Maggie smiled. Perhaps bringing Tiny here hadn't been such a bad idea after all.

Clint slept most of the afternoon and that evening listlessly ate his dinner without complaint. When Maggie checked on him before retiring and discovered him looking flushed and bleary-eyed, she quickly took his temperature. Finding it had inched slightly above one hundred and one, she once again brought him aspirin and a glass of water. Though he grumbled under his breath, this time Clint didn't refuse.

A Texas "blue norther" blew in sometime during the night, sending the temperature plummeting down into the low thirties, its gusting winds stripping the dried brown and gold leaves from the trees.

Maggie returned from her morning jog rosy-cheeked and on top of the world, positively bursting with energy. After she had showered and dressed, she took Clint his breakfast, then set about preparing Thanksgiving dinner. By midday the house was filled with tempting aromas: roasting turkey and cornbread dressing, baking sweet potatoes, pumpkin, mincemeat, and pecan pies. Well aware that she was cooking far more than she and Clint could possibly eat, Maggie told herself she would freeze the leftovers. Thanksgiving simply wasn't Thanksgiving without all the trimmings.

Clint strolled in shortly after noon wearing his ridiculously skimpy robe and helped himself to a cup of coffee.

"Are you ready for lunch?" Maggie asked.

"No. I'll just wait for that feast you're preparing," Clint replied, settling himself at the kitchen table.

A long curl of red peel spiraled down into the sink as Maggie deftly worked a paring knife over an apple. Its sweet, fruity scent rose to mingle with the other delectable aromas filling the room. Glancing over her shoulder at Clint, she frowned and said severely, "You shouldn't be out of bed, you know."

"Staying in bed is driving me crazy," he shot back. "Besides, I think my fever is gone."

Without thinking, Maggie marched over to him and held the back of her hand to his cheek to check for herself. A flame leaped into Clint's eyes, and Maggie caught her breath as his big hand covered hers. His hot breath seemed to scorch her as he turned his head and nibbled the tender skin on the back of her hand. "Maggie," he whispered softly, evocatively, holding her apprehensive gaze with his mesmerizing emerald eyes. The tip of his tongue tasted her, then drew a slow, tantalizing pattern over the delicate flesh, and Maggie shivered.

Panicked, she snatched her hand away, whirled back to the stove and snatched a lid off the pot simmering on the back burner. "Heavens! If I'm not careful I'm going to burn our dinner. And I'm starving. I must have run five miles this morning," she babbled, in an effort to cover her confusion.

She gave the bubbling giblet gravy a quick stir and replaced the lid, then returned to the sink and picked up the half-peeled apple, carefully keeping her back to Clint. How in the world was she supposed to cope when he could turn her into a helpless lump of quivering desire with just a touch, a look? No matter how hard she fought to deny them, her feelings for Clint were growing day by day.

Maggie's chin quivered, and she blinked and widened her eyes to hold back the tears that threatened. *What a fool you are, Maggie Trent. It's stupid, reckless and self-destructive to let yourself care for a man like Clint, and you know it. Probably better than anyone. All you've done is set yourself up for more heartache.* But sadly she accepted that logic, common sense, and past experience were pitifully inadequate weapons against the powerful attraction between them. It was pointless to go on denying it; she was falling in love with this impossible man. Falling, ha! Who was she trying to kid? She was wholeheartedly, passionately, head-over-heels bonkers about him, and had been for weeks. Months probably. *Fool! Fool! Fool!*

Clint got up and refilled his cup, then returned to the table. He reared back in the chair, balancing it on the two back legs. Sipping the aromatic brew, he squinted his eyes against the rising steam and studied Maggie over the rim of the cup.

She was bustling around the kitchen like a fussy little hen, darting back and forth from stove to oven, refrigerator to sink. When she opened the oven door and bent over to check the turkey, his eyes gleamed as they caressed her rounded bottom, the stirring heat in his loins bringing a grim smile of self-derision to his face.

It feels right having her here, he told himself as he tracked her movements around the room. And she looks so right here, flitting around in her socks and her tight little jeans and sweater. Her face was rosy from her exertions, and her hair swung around her face like a shining bell when she moved, and Clint had to fight the urge to snatch her up in his arms and kiss her breathless. The hand that lay against his thigh tightened, his fingers biting into the bunched muscles. Dammit! It *was* right, her being here! Why couldn't he make her see that?

He had known from the beginning that what he felt for Maggie was special, and once he had stopped fighting it, it hadn't taken long for him to fall helplessly, completely in love . . . for the second time in his life. She was lovely, witty, intelligent, maddeningly independent, irritatingly stubborn, and thoroughly adorable, and he'd fight the entire Chinese army single-handed to have her as his own. Clint sighed deeply. On second thought, that might be easier than convincing Maggie to give him a chance. To give *them* a chance.

Why was she fighting him so hard? he asked himself for perhaps the hundredth time. It wasn't all one-sided, and he knew it. It couldn't be, not when she responded to him the way she did. Yet every time he got close to her she panicked and bristled like a porcupine. Why? *Why?*

Searching his mind for an answer to the puzzle, Clint recalled the scornful remarks she had made about the women he dated, and his mouth pursed thoughtfully. Was that it? Was she jealous of the women in his past?

Surely not. After all, he'd been single for five years, and he *was* a man. What did she expect? Although . . . he had to admit, the mere thought of another man touching Maggie made him feel positively murderous.

A gentle smile tugged at Clint's mouth as he watched her open the oven door again and test the dressing with a quick jabbing touch of her finger, the tip of her tongue stuck out of the corner of her mouth in concentration. Sweet heaven! Everything about her delighted him.

What had her exhusband been like? he wondered suddenly. An utter fool, no doubt. He had to have been to let a woman like Maggie get away from him.

When she was his he would never let her go, Clint swore silently, vehemently. And she *would* be his. On that he was determined. Because the thought of going through life without her was unbearable.

Turning, Maggie caught the fierce look on Clint's face and her heart jumped in alarm. "I . . . uh"—her hand fluttered weakly toward the door—"the table in the dining room is set and dinner is almost ready. If you'll excuse me, I'll go upstairs and change."

"I'll go with you," Clint said, rolling to his feet. "If you're going to dress up I certainly can't come to the table in my tatty old bathrobe," he added amiably, confusing her even more.

As they walked side by side up the stairs, Maggie's heart was pounding so hard she was sure he could hear it. The fine hairs on her forearms were standing on end. She felt as though every nerve ending in her body was raw. Exposed. Acutely aware that in her socks she didn't even come up to Clint's shoulder, she was suddenly, illogically overwhelmed by his size. His hand at the back of her waist, guiding her solicitously up the stairs, burned through her thin sweater like a branding iron. With every shallow breath she absorbed the scent of his maleness, overlaid with clean soap and woodsy aftershave, and she realized, rather giddily, that he must have showered and shaved when he woke up from his nap.

Her awareness of him didn't lessen when she entered her room. It was located right next to Clint's, and the slight sounds coming through the wall produced vivid pictures in her mind: pictures of Clint shedding the terrycloth robe and striding nude across the floor, as he had done only yesterday, his magnificent male body rippling with leashed power.

Shivering violently, Maggie snatched the logan green wool dress from its hanger and flung it over her head. With quick, agitated movements, she applied her makeup and brushed her hair, then stepped into a pair of elegant brown suede pumps and fled the room.

The dinner was perfect and Clint was charming, which only made Maggie more nervous. She ate so much that by the end of the meal she was groaning. Even after she had loaded the dishwasher and finished cleaning up the kitchen she was still in misery.

When Maggie entered the living room she expected to find Clint watching one of the many Thanksgiving Day football games on TV. Instead he was stretched out on the sofa covered with a colorful gold, rust, and brown afghan, his head propped on an exquisite bar-gello needlepoint throw pillow. A cheery fire was crackling in the fireplace, and soft, soothing music poured from the stereo speakers hidden somewhere in the corners of the room.

Lifting the forearm that lay across his brow, Clint smiled at her sleepily through half-closed eyes and waved at the chair grouping on the opposite side of the hearth. "Have a seat and join me."

The tranquil setting did nothing to ease Maggie's nervousness, quite the opposite in fact. Warily, she settled herself into one of the overstuffed chairs, kicked off her shoes, and curled her feet beneath her, eyeing Clint suspiciously.

Sighing with contentment, Clint settled himself more comfortably on the oatmeal-colored cushions of the sofa and gave Maggie a warm smile. "This is nice, isn't it?"

"What?"

"Oh, you know . . . the fire, the music, the peace." A pause, then he added in a husky voice that made her heart trip over itself, "Being alone here. Just the two of us."

Maggie was out of the chair like an uncoiling spring. Without thinking, she went to the fireplace, snatched up a poker, and began jabbing needlessly at the dancing fire. "What time does the girls' plane get in Sunday?" she asked, the non sequitur coming out in a nervous, high-pitched voice that betrayed her agitation. "Do you recall?"

"Eight ten," Clint replied, and even with her back to him Maggie could tell he was amused.

Stupid! Don't let him see how much the situation is getting to you, she berated herself severely. It's going to be hard enough getting through the rest of this day without jumping like a startled doe every time the man makes a suggestive remark.

But to Maggie's surprise, and growing unease, Clint behaved like a perfect gentleman. That is, if one didn't count the hot, blatantly sensual look in his eyes every time he so much as glanced in her direction.

As the day wore on and afternoon turned into evening, Clint kept up a steady stream of mainly one-sided conversation. Several times he tried to draw Maggie out, asking questions about her childhood, her preferences in music, literature, and food, but his probing merely made her more on edge, and her replies came out short and curt and completely noncommittal. Drat the man! Maggie ranted silently at his persistence. Why couldn't he just have watched football, like every other normal male over the age of twelve on Thanksgiving Day?

Through the evening, Maggie alternately stirred the fire, squirmed in her chair, and struggled to ignore the husky, caressing quality of Clint's voice and the unmistakable longing in his emerald eyes, to say nothing of the quivering sensation in the pit of her stomach.

Finally, after what seemed like an eternity to Maggie, Clint seemed to tire of his fruitless efforts. He fell silent and, with a sigh, rolled over onto his back, closed his eyes, and draped his forearm across his brow.

A twinge of concern twisted through Maggie at the sight of him. He was probably feeling very weak and washed out. He was certainly exhausted, if the lines of strain around his mouth were anything to go by. Perhaps she should have insisted that he stay in bed today?

Helplessly, longingly, her eyes devoured him, inching hungrily over the brawny, masculine frame, noticing how large and powerful yet strangely graceful his hands were with their long, blunt fingers and squared-off, well-kept nails, the way the short black hairs shadowed his forearms and the back of his hands. She watched the slow rise and fall of his massive chest, feeling her own tighten painfully. His shoulders were impossibly broad, his abdomen a flat plane of hard muscle and firm flesh. She remembered how he looked naked, and desire raced through her in a hot, shimmering wave. Maggie clenched her teeth against it, and the hands in her lap curled into tight, white-knuckled fists. Heaven help her, she couldn't take much more of this torment!

"What are you thinking, Maggie?" Clint asked quietly from the sofa, and she looked at him in faint alarm. Had her expression given her away?

"I was thinking that you're looking better," she improvised quickly. "Your spots are much less noticeable. They should be gone completely by morning. If your fever is gone, too, then I'll take Tiny and get out of your way."

"You don't have to go, Maggie."

The softly issued statement sent a quiver of longing through Maggie, but she struggled valiantly to suppress it. "Of course I do. The only reason I came was because you were ill and needed someone to look after you."

"Was it?"

"Yes!" she snapped, unnerved by the soft probing and the warm, intimate look in his eyes. "I would have done the same for anyone." The war of emotions within her was tearing Maggie apart. She yearned with every fiber of her being to give in to her feelings, to throw herself into Clint's arms and experience the pleasure she knew she would find there, to let her love flow, natural and free . . . but she didn't dare. Nothing had changed. She couldn't accept anything but absolute fidelity from the man she loved . . . and Clint was incapable of giving it.

Swallowing against the painful tightness in her throat, she rose jerkily to her feet. "Now, if you'll excuse me, I'm very tired. I think I'll go to my room."

"Maggie, don't go! It's early yet!"

Maggie ignored his frantic call, and Clint watched in grim frustration as she all but ran from the room. Loyally, Tiny hauled himself up from his comfortable spot by the hearth, stretched hugely, and started after her. At the door he paused to give the distraught man on the sofa a soulful look, then whined softly and, head down, trailed after his mistress.

Clint sat up, throwing the afghan aside, a string of

softly vicious oaths pouring from him. Leaning forward, he propped his elbows on his knees and cradled his head in his hands. What was he going to do? He couldn't let her leave tomorrow. He couldn't! This weekend was a heaven-sent opportunity, and besides, he had a terrible, gut feeling that if he didn't break through that wall Maggie had placed around her heart soon, he never would.

Groaning, Clint raked both hands through his hair. He had to *do* something.

For what seemed like the hundredth time, Maggie raised up on one elbow and punched her pillow into a different shape. But it was no use. She simply could not sleep. She had tried a hot shower. She had tried pacing the floor. She'd even tried counting sheep. But nothing seemed to work.

Staring at the ceiling, she wondered if Clint was having trouble sleeping too. She doubted it. Shortly after she had come upstairs he had followed, and for a few minutes she had heard him stirring about . . . then nothing. A quick glance at the bedside clock told her that had been almost two hours ago. Angrily, she flounced over onto her side and stared into the darkness. How could that insensitive clod sleep, knowing she was in the next room? It was downright insulting.

At first she thought she had imagined the sound. Then she heard it again; a low groan, muffled by the thickness of the wall.

In a split second Maggie was out of the bed and flying across the room toward the door. The frilly lavender nightgown billowed out behind her like a ship's sail as her bare feet raced the short distance to Clint's door. Not bothering to knock, she flung it open and tore across the room to the bed.

Clint lay on his back, perfectly still. Cautiously,

Maggie bent over his recumbent form and peered down at him.

"Oh!"

The startled yelp burst out as steely hands grasped her upper arms and jerked her downward. In the next instant Maggie found herself sprawled inelegantly on top of Clint's broad, hair-covered chest.

"Oh, you—you *sneak!*" Maggie cried in outrage. "There's nothing wrong with you! You lured me in here on purpose to—to . . ."

"To bring you to your senses and prove to you, once and for all, that this is where you belong: in my arms and in my bed," Clint growled with sensual menace.

Maggie sucked in her breath, so astounded at his unmitigated gall all she could do was stare at him for a full five seconds. "Why you arrogant, conceited oaf! Who the devil do you think you are? Let me go!" she railed, pummeling his chest with her fists. "Let me go this instant, you devious, conniving—"

The vitriolic tirade was pushed back into her throat as Clint rolled her over onto her back and captured her mouth with his. Maggie was taken so completely by surprise she never even had a chance.

His big body blanketed her, pressing her deep into the mattress. His lips were warm and insistent, tasting and devouring her with a hungry, demanding passion that would not be denied.

A strangled sound of protest issued from Maggie's throat, and she shoved at Clint's chest, but it was like trying to lift a mountain. You've got to stop him. You can't let this happen, she told herself urgently, even as she felt her body go all weak and warm with longing. But it was no use. She could no more resist him than she could fly, and finally, with an anguished moan that was part anger and part undeniable pleasure, Maggie's ineffectual struggles ceased. The needs of her heart and her body were too great. She went boneless under his warm weight, her lips softening instinctively against the insistent pressure of his mouth.

Her response brought a low groan from Clint, and his tongue slid into the sweet warmth to entwine with hers. The kiss grew deeper, more intense as each tasted the very essence of the other, drinking deeply, like two souls long denied.

Easing his embrace, Clint shifted to his side, until he was only partially covering her. Stringing moist kisses and impassioned love words over her cheek, he forged a path to her ear. Maddeningly, his tongue traced the delicate swirls, then he buried his face against her smooth, scented neck while his hands began a restless, intimate exploration, stroking her from breast to hip to knee, and back again.

A violent shiver rippled through Maggie, and her hands flexed against his muscular chest, her fingers burying themselves in the mat of crisp hair. The heat from his body was searing her through the thin silk gown, and dimly Maggie realized that Clint was naked. Nipping greedily at his smooth shoulders, she allowed her hand to slide around his ribcage and, with delicate savagery, dug her nails into the broad, rippling muscles of his back. An indescribable thrill shot through Maggie as she felt his quivering reaction.

"Oh, sweet heaven, love, you feel so good," Clint whispered into the hollow at the base of her neck. He placed tiny, moist kisses along the delicate curve of her collarbone, then his tongue trailed a path of fire down into the silken valley exposed by the plunging V neckline of her gown. Nuzzling his face against her, he breathed deeply. "You smell like sunshine and flowers. A man could go crazy just holding you."

His fingers slid beneath the delicate material and nudged it aside to curve possessively around her full, warm breast, while his mouth began a slow, tantalizing climb up over the pearly mound. Moaning, Maggie arched her back, shivering violently as his tongue stroked over her swollen nipple.

Clint's hand glided downward over the silky night-gown to rest on her flat, quivering belly. Slowly, he lifted his head and gazed down at her. His eyes were almost black with desire, and his features were flushed with passion. His big hand covered her abdomen completely, his fingertips cupping one hip, his thumb the other. "Dear God, Maggie," he murmured thickly. "You're so tiny, I'm almost afraid to touch you." His eyes lifted and met hers with fiery intent. "But I won't hurt you, sweetheart. I swear it." A tremor shook his hand when it lifted slowly to ease the gown down over her hips. "Oh, Maggie," he groaned as he felt her stir against him. "I've wanted you so long. So very long. Ever since that first night when you walked in here with Allison and Laura, I've wanted you."

That first night? When he'd had that Bunny creature here? Even then he had wanted to add me to his lists of conquests? The very thought sent a wave of sickness through Maggie, and she stiffened in his arms. What was she *doing,* letting him seduce her like this? Had she lost her *mind?*

With a sudden twist of her body that took Clint completely by surprise, Maggie wrenched free of his arms and rolled from the bed. Backing away from him, fumbling desperately to pull her gown back into place, she shook her head emphatically, her eyes wide and desperate. "No! No, I won't let you do this to me! Just stay away from me, Clinton Rafferty. Just stay away," she cried hysterically as she whirled away from the astonished man on the bed and fled out the door.

Maggie gave no thought to where she was going. She just ran. Out the door, along the hall, down the stairs, through the entry—her feet carried her without conscious direction. When at last she stopped she was leaning over the kitchen sink, breathing hard, her heart pounding. Tears blurred her vision, and she struggled to hold them back, but it was wasted effort. They flowed over her lashes and plopped into the enameled sink, bouncing and splattering like raindrops. Terrible, wrenching sobs forced their way up her tight throat, shaking her slight frame as she stood gripping the edge of the sink, her face twisted in anguish.

Why? Why can't I fall for some nice, reliable man? Why does it always have to be some faithless, philandering charmer? Maggie's head came up, and her chin quivered as she struggled to get a grip on her emotions. No. No, I won't love him. I won't! she vowed.

Fists hit the kitchen door, and it flew open, crashing back against the adjacent cabinets with a startling bang, and causing Maggie to jump and cry out in alarm.

"Maggie, what the hell is going on?" Clint thundered, coming to a halt in the middle of the kitchen. "If this is a game you're playing, it's not amusing."

Maggie swung around and pressed back against the sink, a hunted look in her wide blue eyes. "It's no game," she declared with shaky defiance. "I want you to leave me alone."

"Liar!" Clint stated succinctly, rudely. "I wasn't the only one breathing heavily just a minute ago. Lady, you wanted me as much as I wanted you. Don't you dare try to deny it."

"I . . . I'm not trying to deny it." A self-derisive grimace contorted Maggie's features and she shook her head. "I can't." She looked up then, her face becoming stony with determination as she met his angry glare. "But I *will not* let myself become involved with you, Clint. Do you hear me? Never again will I let myself be hurt by a man like you."

"Hurt?" Clint looked at her as though she'd lost her mind. "I'd never hurt you," he insisted in a stunned voice. "And what the hell do you mean, 'a man like me'?"

"I mean a man who can't be satisfied with just one woman. A man who has to prove his masculinity by jumping into bed with every female he sees. Oh, don't give me that shocked look!" she flared, her temper overcoming her hurt. "Don't forget, I've seen you in action with Bunny. And Lisa. And I've heard all about your set of interchangeable girlfriends from Allison, so you can just knock off the wounded innocent act!"

Clint opened his mouth to speak, but Maggie cut him off. "I was married to a man just like you for eleven years." She looked him up and down, her face full of scorn. "He was a football hero, too, only injuries kept him out of the pros. He was charming and handsome and utterly faithless. It was humiliating and degrading to realize that your husband, the man who claimed to love you, was sleeping with anything in skirts. And if that weren't bad enough, every year his women got younger and younger." Maggie's chin came up. "Well never again. I have no intention of ever finding myself in that kind of situation again."

Every trace of anger was gone from Clint's face. His gaze held only understanding and compassion and great tenderness. He lifted his hands and very gently framed her face, brushing his thumbs across her tear-stained cheeks. His voice was soft and soothing, caressing, caring. "I'm not like your exhusband, Maggie," he assured her tenderly. "I was very much in love with my wife, and in the ten years we were married I was never once unfaithful to her. I was never even tempted. When she died, I wanted to die too, and I was positive that I could never care that much for another woman again." He smiled wryly and shrugged his shoulders. "I think, deep down inside, just the thought of making that kind of emotional commitment to another woman made me feel guilty. Unfaithful to her memory. Sooo . . . I only went out with young, good-time girls who could satisfy my physical needs but never touch my heart."

He saw the flicker of uncertainty and hope in Maggie's eyes and slipped his big hands farther around her head, his fingers tunneling deep into the brown silk hair. Exerting just the slightest pressure, he pulled her closer and tilted her face up until she was forced to look directly into his eyes. "But you were different, Maggie," he insisted softly, forcefully. "I knew from the first moment we met that you were going to be important to me." He sighed and his mouth twisted ruefully. "I fought against it at first, but it was no use. My feelings for you are inescapable." His hands tightened their grip, and his gaze held hers captive. "Since the moment you walked into my house that night there has been no other woman in my life. I swear it."

Maggie made an impatient sound and shifted restlessly. "Surely you don't expect me to believe that," she scoffed. "What about Bunny? And Lisa?"

"I took Bunny home right after you left. As for Lisa, I'm ashamed to say, I was using her. I knew you were going to be at Renauldo's that night, and I asked her out so I would have an excuse to go there." His voice was firm and controlled. His expression was open. Not even Maggie could doubt he was telling the truth.

Hope welled inside her like a bubbling spring, but she held it firmly in check. Biting her lower lip, she looked at him with uncertainty. She wanted to believe him. She wanted to believe him so badly it hurt . . . yet still the doubts persisted.

"Trust me, darling," Clint urged gently. "I won't hurt you." He tilted his head to the side and cocked one brow. "You *do* believe me don't you?"

At Maggie's slow nod a wide smile spread over his face. "Good," he sighed with satisfaction. "Now, before we go any further, is there anything else bothering you. Any other little reason why you think we shouldn't become involved? If so, let's get it out in the open right now."

Never far from the surface, Maggie's normal good humor was beginning to reassert itself, and she looked up at him slyly and blinked. She pursed her lips and puckered her forehead into a doubtful frown, letting her fingers absently walk up over his chest, pausing now and then to pluck at the curling chest hairs between the lapels of his robe.

"We-ellll . . . there is this one problem," she said dubiously, and Clint's smile quickly turned into a frown.

"What?" he demanded, clamping his hand over her wandering fingers.

Wrinkling her nose impudently, Maggie sighed and replied, "You're much too tall for me."

Clint's eyes narrowed into glittering green slits. "Oh, I wouldn't worry about that, sweetheart," he drawled in a dangerous, velvety voice, and without warning his big hands encircled her waist to lift her effortlessly onto the counter. Maggie gasped and clutched at his hair as he buried his face between her breasts. Against her soft, scented skin he murmured tauntingly, "I think you'll find that I'm very inventive."

Chapter Eight

The feel of warm lips nibbling their way up the side of her neck pulled Maggie from her pleasant dream. She stirred in sleepy irritation, but undeterred the marauding mouth continued its exploration. Slowly, Maggie opened her eyes and blinked. The first thing that came into focus was a brawny, hair-covered, definitely masculine forearm . . . right in front of her nose.

"Morning, sleepyhead," came Clint's throaty whisper when she hunched her shoulder and turned her head to look up at him. He was leaning over her, smiling, an arm braced on each side of her head. His eyes ran over her sleep-softened features lovingly, his expression full of tenderness and sensuality and unmistakable male possessiveness. "Since you won't let me sleep with you, the least you could do is wake up and keep me company," he teased. "Besides, it's time for our morning run."

Maggie smiled and turned over to twine her arms

around his neck. This was even better than her dream. Then, as his words soaked into her fuzzy brain she blinked and frowned. "What do you mean 'our' run? You're not going. You're not well enough yet."

"If you go, I go," he informed her, winding a strand of her shining hair around his forefinger. "Of course . . . if you want to skip it this morning, I won't complain." He dipped his head and mouthed the tender skin on the underside of her jaw. "We could always stay right here."

"Clint, stop that." Her voice throaty with the first stirrings of passion, the words came out more a quavering plea than a command. Maggie shivered deliciously as she felt his hand slide up over her ribcage to cup the underside of her breast. His warmth penetrated the silk gown as though it didn't exist, igniting a fire deep inside her that suffused her entire body with heat.

"Do you really want me to stop?" he questioned plaintively, nuzzling the delicate hollows at the base of her throat.

"N–no I don't, but . . . but we must," she stammered, forcing the words out. "Besides, you . . . you promised."

Clint sucked in a deep, chest expanding breath, held it, then let it go in a long sigh. Straightening slowly, he looked down at her and shook his head wryly. "You're really going to hold me to that, aren't you?"

Pulling the sheet up over her breasts, Maggie eyed him cautiously and nodded, and Clint groaned.

"You're a hard-hearted woman, Maggie Trent, but if that's the way it's got to be . . ." He let the sentence trail away as he rose to his feet. Resignation stamped his features, but his gaze was warm. "Well? What will it be, jogging"—he paused, his eyes gleaming with anticipation, brows waggling enticingly—"or a big breakfast of sausage and pancakes, with lots of butter and boysenberry syrup, and orange juice and milk and coffee and—"

"Enough! Enough!" Maggie held up both hands, palms outward. "You're corrupting me, you terrible man! You know I can't resist a breakfast like that."

Clint laughed and started for the door. "Don't worry about it, sweetheart. When I'm completely well I'll run you an extra five miles around the park to make up for it."

When he had gone Maggie stretched sensuously and smiled up at the ceiling for no reason. It was almost impossible to resist that man. How she had done it last night, she hadn't the slightest idea. When he had lifted her up onto the counter and pressed his face against her breasts, she had almost fainted with pleasure. But somehow she had managed to hold onto a modicum of common sense. A tingle raced through Maggie as she closed her eyes and recalled the delicious sensations his touch had evoked.

"Clint. Clint, I . . . I can't," she had whispered raggedly, clutching his head between her hands, her fingers buried deep in the midnight dark curls. "We must stop."

"Why? We want each other. We're right for each other. For God's sake, Maggie, let me love you." Eyes closed, he breathed the words against her skin, and Maggie shivered in ecstasy as his warm, moist breath caressed her.

Desperately, she gritted her teeth and summoned up the strength to deny him . . . to deny them both. "Clint, listen to me." Applying pressure, she lifted his head and forced him to look at her. "There's not just the two of us involved here. We both have daughters to think of. Very young daughters. Don't you see? I have to set an example for Laura. I can't tell her to behave one way while I behave the opposite, no matter how I feel."

Clint opened his mouth as though to argue, then closed it again. Frustrated, he stared back at her, his face taut and strained. She could see his inner struggle in his eyes, the warring emotions that were tearing him apart; he wanted her, but he knew she was right.

"All right," he sighed resignedly. "I see your point. But where does that leave us?"

Maggie's eyes grew soft, and tenderly she combed her fingers through the hair at his temples. "Couldn't we just take some time to get to know each other? To be sure where this relationship is going, before we commit ourselves?"

It wasn't what he wanted to hear, and Maggie could see it in his eyes, but finally, his face grim, he muttered, "Okay. We'll play it cool for a while. But only for a while," he added warningly.

As she threw back the covers and started for the bathroom, Maggie wondered just how long Clint's "a while" was. Not terribly long, she was sure.

Standing beneath the hot, stinging shower spray, Maggie felt an effervescent joy bubbling up inside her, and though she told herself not to get carried away, that it was much, much too soon to be sure of anything, the feeling did not lessen. With the memory of last night still fresh and buoyant in her mind, nothing could subdue her good spirits. Her chest was tight with anticipation, and she felt alive and eager and on top of the world. When she stepped from the shower she was glowing, her cheeks flushed with inner excitement, her eyes a clear sparkling blue. Leaning close to the mirror, Maggie inspected her reflection and smiled. Without a doubt, being in love was the best beauty treatment in the world. "If I could just bottle it and sell it I'd be a billionaire," she chirped happily, patting herself dry.

Fifteen minutes later, dressed in a teal blue sweater with raglan sleeves and cream wool slacks, sans shoes, Maggie entered the kitchen to find Clint at the stove, his back to her. The coffee maker gurgled as the glass pot slowly filled with brown liquid, its tantalizing aroma mingling with the delicious scents of sizzling sausage and browning pancakes.

Maggie paused just inside the door and watched Clint for a moment. He was whistling merrily while, with a deft flick of his wrist, one by one he flipped each pancake up in the air and caught it in a plate, all with the panache and self-confidence of a man who is totally at ease and secure within himself. Maggie shook her head in mild amazement, a tender smile on her face. Never in a million years would Larry have prepared her breakfast. He considered cooking and household chores "woman's work," and to even suggest that he do them was an insult to his masculinity.

But there was nothing even remotely feminine about Clint's broad-shouldered back, narrow hips, and long, muscular thighs. Unable to resist, Maggie walked up behind him and slipped both arms around his middle.

"Ummmm, I like that," Clint murmured throatily as she nestled against his back, the top of her head fitting just between his shoulder blades.

"So do I." With a sigh, Maggie hugged closer and, rubbing her cheek against the soft flannel of his shirt, made a sound very like a purr.

Clint turned slowly within the circle of her embrace and wrapped his arms around her. He bent his head, and Maggie looped her arms around his neck, raised up on tiptoes, and lifted her mouth to his. The kiss was soft and warm. With unhurried ease they savored one another, tongues stroking, tasting, lips caressing. They swayed together dreamily, hearts pounding with a slow, heavy beat, each relishing the freedom to touch, to taste, to experience the other's closeness.

Their lips clung, then slowly parted. For a moment Maggie remained as she was, head thrown back, eyes closed, lips parted and wet. Then, with drowsy sensuality, she lifted her lids part way and met his smoldering gaze.

"Clint?" she whispered.

Clint's answering smile was indulgent, amused, full of male confidence and sensual promise. "What, love?" he inquired, rocking her suggestively against his hips.

Blinking slowly, Maggie sighed, and in her sexiest voice, replied, "The sausage is burning," then promptly dissolved in a fit of laughter when Clint let out a shocking string of oaths and spun around to rescue their breakfast.

He lifted the browned patties from the skillet and placed them on the waiting, paper towel–covered plate, slanting her a look that was a mixture of exasperation and amusement. "Go ahead and laugh, you little devil," he growled menacingly. "But don't think I'm going to forget this. Your time is coming."

His threat had no effect whatever on Maggie's good spirits. Breakfast and the rest of the day passed in a pleasant round of teasing and laughter, interspersed with warm looks and frequent stolen kisses.

The disparity in their sizes proved no obstacle for Clint. The man was not just inventive when it came to overcoming the problem—he was downright brilliant! Maggie found herself being kissed sitting on the kitchen counter, the backs of chairs, the piano—any place that was high enough to bring her up to his level. Every time she started up the stairs, she no sooner set foot on the bottom step than she was spun around and kissed soundly. When there was nothing convenient to sit her on, Clint solved the problem merely by picking her up and holding her against his chest. And of course, the sitting and prone positions offered no problem at all; draped across his lap or stretched out beside him on the rug, Maggie's size was of no importance.

All that marred the day, as far as Maggie was concerned, were the frequent calls Clint received. That the callers were women she had no doubt. Men didn't use that low, soft tone on other men. To be perfectly fair, Clint's manner was never flirtatious or intimate, and he always ended the calls quickly, but still Maggie's irritation grew . . . along with her doubts. She tried to tell herself that she was being unreasonable, that until last night Clint had been a free agent, and even now there had been no commitment made on either side. It didn't help.

By the fifth call Maggie was doing a slow burn. When the phone rang again while they were preparing dinner, she had to grind her teeth to hold in the comment that hovered on the tip of her tongue.

Giving her an apologetic smile, Clint put down the lettuce he was breaking apart for a salad and wiped his hands on a towel, then crossed to the wall phone and lifted the receiver.

"Hello."

From the corner of her eye Maggie watched his face for some sign of irritation. When none was forthcoming she pressed her mouth into a thin line and severed the base of a stalk of broccoli with one sharp whack of the butcher knife.

"No, I'm sorry," Clint said to the person on the other end of the line. "I can't make it tonight."

No, I'm sorry. I can't make it tonight, Maggie mimicked silently. Why don't you just tell her you're not available anymore? Or is that too final for you?

"Yes, I'm sure it's going to be a great party, and I'm sorry I'll have to miss it, but it just can't be helped. I have another engagement. One I can't break." Clint turned to Maggie, but she was too busy hacking away at the broccoli to notice the tender smile he gave her.

Oh, by all means, don't let me stand in your way, she fumed to herself, attacking the hapless vegetable as though it were a vicious animal that had threatened her life. I certainly wouldn't want to put a crimp in your style.

Clint chuckled softly at something the woman said, then repeated. "No. I can't. Look, Bunny, I've told you three times already today that I can't take you to that party. You're just going to have to get someone else."

Bunny? *Bunny?* Maggie slammed the knife down on the counter. That did it! She wasn't about to stand here one more minute and listen to him pacify that silly creature! Spinning on her heel, she turned and stalked toward the door.

When she drew level with Clint he smiled and tried to slip his arm around her, but she dodged away and sent him a withering glare. Head high, face set, she moved haughtily past him but was jerked to a halt from behind when he rammed his hand into the waistband of her slacks and held on. Maggie struggled to break free, but it was like being on a treadmill; her feet and legs were moving but she was going nowhere.

"Let me go!" she hissed, reaching around to pry his hand loose from her clothing.

Clint put an end to her rebellion by merely lifting her clear of the floor. "I'm sorry, Bunny. What did you say?" he asked pleasantly, as Maggie dangled helplessly at the end of his arm.

"Put me down, you beast!" Maggie screeched. Her arms and legs were flailing the air like an awkward swimmer in imminent danger of drowning. "Put me down this instant!"

"Stop that," Clint ordered, giving her a little shake when she began to pound his kneecap with her fist. "What? Oh, no, not you, Bunny. I was talking to someone else."

Maggie was beyond rational thought. The indignity of being dangled in the air enraged her so she could only react. The only part of Clint's anatomy within reach of her retribution was his leg, and she wasted no time launching her attack. Hooking a hand around his knee, Maggie pulled herself in close and sank her teeth into his thigh.

"No, Bunny, I ca—*aaaaahhh!*"

Clint dropped Maggie like a hot potato and grabbed his wounded leg with both hands. The phone receiver plunged nearly to the floor on its coiled cord, then slammed against the wall, and Maggie hit the floor in a spread-eagled belly flop that drove the breath from her body in a loud whoosh. She lay dazed. Clint danced around on one leg, turning the air blue with livid curses before finally overbalancing and crashing to the floor. From the swinging receiver, bumping rhythmically against the wall, came the high-pitched, tinny sound of Bunny's voice calling Clint's name.

Clint glowered blackly at Maggie. "Dammit Maggie! What the hell's the matter with you?" he roared. "You nearly bit a chunk out of my leg!"

Rolling over onto her back, Maggie groaned, raised up on her elbows, drew in several, deep, painful breaths, and glowered back. "When you're small you learn to use whatever means available to fend off bullies," she returned.

Clint's eyes narrowed on her. "I wasn't bullying you. I was merely trying to stop you from stomping off in a huff. Now listen to me, Maggie, just because . . . Oh no you don't!" he growled forcefully, making a diving lunge for her when she attempted to rise. Using his superior weight he held her squirming body captive and pinned her wrists to the floor on either side of her head. Nose to nose they glared at one another, until finally Maggie ceased her futile struggles.

"All right. That's better," Clint said with blatant male satisfaction that made Maggie's blood boil. "Now, as I was saying, there is no reason for you to be upset just because I was talking to Bunny on the phone. She means nothing to me, but I'm not a completely insensitive brute. If I can let her down easy without hurting her, I will. Eventually she'll get the message that I'm just not interested." He read the uncertainty in Maggie's expression and his own softened. He smiled down at her, his eyes warm and loving. "You have no reason to be jealous, darling. You're the only woman in my life. The only one I want in my life," he assured her tenderly. "Though I will admit, it's nice to know you care. Nice . . . but painful," he added with a rueful grimace, releasing one of her hands for a moment to gingerly rub his abused leg.

"I am *not* jealous," she denied haughtily.

"Sure you are." Clint lowered his head and captured her mouth with his. The kiss was soft and persuasive, and infinitely sensual. When he pulled back to look down at her, his eyes were glowing with a mixture of amusement and desire. "Come on," he urged, his voice a husky whisper. "Admit it. You were jealous."

Maggie opened her mouth to deny it, hesitated, then closed it again. "Oh, all right," she conceded grudgingly. "Maybe I was just a bit jealous."

"Only a bit?"

"Yes!"

"Liar."

He chuckled at her outraged sputtering and lowered his head once again.

On principle Maggie strained against the embrace, but it was a half-hearted attempt at best, and after a moment her struggles ceased. Feeling the resistance drain out of her, Clint released her hands, and immediately they lifted to curve around the back of his head and draw him closer. With a growl of satisfaction, he shifted to one side and cupped a breast in his palm, his thumb sweeping back and forth across its hardening peak in a slow, tantalizing motion.

The kiss was both tender and passionate, soft and demanding, greedy and giving. Legs entangled, they strained together in desperate need, lost to the world around them. Neither was aware of the hard floor beneath them, the small, distant voice still shrilling from the dangling telephone receiver, the faint smell of something burning on the stove . . . or the sudden click-click of canine toenails against the tile floor.

But they were soon made aware of Tiny's presence. Entering the kitchen, the huge dog spied the entwined couple on the floor and was instantly intent on joining the fun. Barking delightedly, he circled them twice, then, in an excess of enthusiasm, proceeded to jump on top of them.

Clint let out a roar of outrage that sent the dog scrambling for cover, while Maggie dissolved in a fit of laughter.

"That misplaced sense of humor is going to get you murdered one of these days. You know that don't you?"

Clint's threatening growl only made Maggie laugh harder, and with a disgusted groan, he rolled onto his back and scowled at the ceiling.

With an effort Maggie finally brought her laughter

under control and turned on her side to watch him, lips twitching. His profile remained rock hard. Reaching out with one hand, she very daringly ran her forefinger over the hard line of his mouth. "It *was* funny, though, wasn't it," she wheedled, in a voice that still vibrated with suppressed amusement.

"Funny, hell! I must have been nuts when I suggested you bring that monster here."

"Grouch," she taunted softly.

After a moment Clint turned his head and met her twinkling gaze with a stern look, but try as he may he couldn't prevent his mouth from turning upward. "Oh, all right," he grumbled at last. "So it *was* funny. That dog is still a menace."

The days that followed were both a joy and pure torture. It was heaven to be around Clint constantly, to have him all to herself. Their feelings for one another grew steadily as they shared both laughter and quiet, serious moments. Clint was a good listener, and Maggie found herself telling him things she had never told another living soul. Slowly she began to realize that she was extremely happy, happier than she had ever thought possible. Yet, at the same time, it was sheer hell. She loved Clint more every day, and though he never said it, she was sure he felt the same. As that love grew, so did their passion for one another, and the strain of not allowing that passion to reach fulfillment was almost intolerable.

All too soon Sunday night arrived and it was time to go to the airport. They had agreed that until things were settled between them they would be discreet in front of the girls. When Laura and Allison emerged from the boarding tunnel, Maggie and Clint were standing side by side, not touching, the air between them crackling with awareness.

They greeted their daughters with hugs and kisses and, after assuring them that Clint was fine, asked about their weekend. All the way to the baggage claim area both girls babbled enthusiastically while Clint and Maggie cast surreptitious glances at one another that spoke volumes.

I miss you already, Maggie's eyes said over the top of Laura's head.

I miss you, too. I don't want to let you go, Clint's replied tenderly.

When they reached the lower level and the girls volunteered to retrieve their luggage from the conveyer belt neither parent objected, each grateful for the opportunity of just a few more minutes together.

"Are you picking up the vibes I'm picking up?" Allison asked excitedly the moment they were out of Clint and Maggie's hearing. "I don't know what happened while we were gone, but those two are positively besotted with one another."

Laura did a little jig and squeezed her friend's arm. "I know. I know. Ooohh, I just can't believe it. Success at last!"

The smug looks on Allison's and Laura's faces when they returned with their bags made Maggie uneasy, but during the ride home they talked of nothing but the parade and the weekend with Dennis and his family. By the time Clint turned the car into her drive Maggie had begun to relax somewhat.

Just inside the front door Allison grabbed Laura's suitcase and announced, "Come on. I'll help you with your things." Without giving the startled girl a chance to reply, she hustled her up the stairs. On the second-floor landing Allison paused and looked down knowingly at Maggie and Clint.

"If you two want to tell each other good night or anything, don't worry about us interrupting. We'll cough real loud before we come down," she said with a conspiratorial wink.

Stunned, the couple in the foyer goggled as the two smug teenagers disappeared around the corner. Slowly, Maggie and Clint turned to look at one another, their faces blank with astonishment. Then both burst out laughing.

"So much for being discreet," Maggie choked at last, leaning weakly against Clint's chest.

Actually, as Maggie was to discover over the next two weeks, it was a relief to have everything out in the open. She and Clint were now free to see each other whenever they wanted, which turned out to be almost every night. In addition, the girls' obvious delight over their parents' new relationship eased Maggie's mind somewhat, and gradually, cautiously, her optimism grew.

Some evenings Maggie and Clint went out to dinner, while other times they just enjoyed quiet evenings at home. Frequently Clint took the four of them out—to dinner, to movies, to ball games, or sometimes just shopping—and though Maggie tried to tell herself not to imagine things or get her hopes up, the feeling that they had somehow become a family continued to grow stronger. If at times she still experienced twinges of doubt about Clint's playboy past, she quickly smothered them. After all, no one could ask for a more attentive or patient suitor.

The one worry Maggie could not ignore or push aside was the upcoming second survey. It loomed like a dark cloud on the horizon, affecting both her professional and personal life. Their relationship shouldn't be a factor in Clint's final decision, she knew, yet Maggie could not help but wonder how she would feel, how she would react, if he did withdraw the Sporting Chance sponsorship from her show.

As it turned out, all Maggie's fears were for nothing.

"I can't believe it," she gasped, sinking down into one of the chairs in front of J.D.'s desk. Her eyes were fixed on the tally sheet she held in her hand. "This is even better than I'd hoped for."

"I don't know why you should be so surprised," her boss chided with a self-satisfied smile, leaning back in his chair and lacing his fingers together over his paunch. "I knew all the time you could pull it off. Why do you think I gave you the go-ahead?"

"J.D.'s right, Maggie. You did a terrific job."

Maggie sent Alex a grateful smile of thanks while prudently curbing the urge to remind J.D. of his earlier opposition to her suggestions.

The relief she felt left her weak in the knees. She had arrived at the station in a high state of nerves, knowing this morning's conference with Henry, Clint, and Selene would have a profound effect on her future. She had been dreading it with every fiber in her being . . . and now this. It was like a miracle! They had made impressive gains in every category!

She barely had time to assimilate her good fortune when J.D.'s secretary ushered in Clint and the others. At Maggie's insistence she and Clint had kept their personal relationship strictly personal, and other than Selene, no one at the station or in Clint's firm knew they were anything but business acquaintances. When he greeted her with a smile and a friendly handshake, as he had the others, only Maggie was aware of the extra little squeeze he gave her hand, or the warm, caressing glint in his eyes.

J.D. wasted no time in getting down to business. The moment the greetings were over and everyone had taken a seat, he handed each of the new arrivals a copy of the survey results and sat back to wait for their reactions, his expression smugly confident.

Maggie sat straight and taut in her chair, her fingers torturing the sheet of paper in her hands. She was barely aware of Selene's pleased murmur or Henry's more boisterous bellow of approval. Her eyes were glued on Clint's face.

Not a hint of expression was betrayed on his rugged features as he studied the report. Maggie hadn't the slightest idea whether he was pleased or disappointed, and as the seconds ticked by her nerves stretched tighter and tighter. She had almost reached screaming point when finally he lifted his head. Slowly, deliberately, his eyes sought and held hers, and in their green depths was a warm glow of pride and approval that made Maggie's heart turn over.

"If you have those contracts handy, I'd like to sign them," he announced quietly, his gaze still fixed on Maggie.

The actual signing was accomplished quickly, in an atmosphere of enthusiastic backslapping and congratulations, and afterward they all adjourned to a nearby restaurant for an early celebration lunch.

Though Clint managed to secure the seat beside her on the plush banquette and spent the entire time rubbing his leg against hers and caressing her thigh under cover of the tablecloth, to Maggie's disappointment there wasn't a single opportunity for so much as a moment alone.

Consolingly, as she and Selene made their way back to the station after lunch, Maggie told herself that it didn't matter, that Clint was sure to call her later in the day with plans for the evening. A private celebration dinner seemed a must.

"So, tell me, how's the romance going?" Selene queried when they had settled down in Maggie's office. She watched Maggie carefully stir a spoonful of powdered cream substitute into her coffee, then cross to her desk and curl one stocking-clad foot under her as she sank down into her swivel chair, cradling the steaming mug between both hands. "You two were certainly playing it cool all morning. That is, if you don't count all that groping under the table at lunch."

Maggie's eyes opened wide in faint alarm. "How did you know?"

"Darling, the gleam in Clint's eyes every time his hand disappeared from view was a dead giveaway," Selene drawled, smiling wickedly at the blush that crept up Maggie's neck and flooded over her face. "But if it's any comfort to you, I don't think the others noticed. They were too busy congratulating each other. Though why you should want to keep your relationship a secret is beyond me. I mean, sweetie, the man is obviously nuts about you. What are you worried about?"

Maggie took a quick swallow of coffee then shrugged her shoulders, her mouth twisting wryly. "I don't know."

"Do you still worry that there are other women in his life?" Selene probed gently.

"Yes . . . no . . . oh, I don't know!" Maggie took another deep swallow from the mug, then sat it on the table and raked the fingers of both hands through her hair. Sighing deeply, she looked at her friend, her eyes brimming with confusion.

"It's just that everything seems so perfect, so right. I keep waiting for the bubble to burst." She stopped and waved her hand in a frustrated gesture. "I guess it all just seems too good to be true. I keep remembering—"

"Maggie, don't do this to yourself," Selene interrupted with quiet urgency. When Maggie looked up every trace of amusement had vanished from the older woman's face, and Selene was watching her intently, her brows drawn together in a concerned frown. "Clinton Rafferty is nothing at all like Larry Trent. I don't know why you can't see that."

A wan smile pulled at Maggie's mouth. Selene had never liked Larry, not from the moment she met him, and over the years had been very vocal about her feelings. Yet all along she had sung Clint's praises. When Selene had dropped by the house one night and accidentally discovered that Maggie and Clint were seeing one another socially, she had been delighted. Could she be right? Was Selene a better judge of men, and their character, than she? Maggie wanted to believe it, but still . . .

The ringing of the phone cut across Maggie's musings, and she snatched it up instantly, unaware of the melting look that crossed her face at the sound of Clint's voice.

"Hi, babe. I miss you," he murmured seductively in her ear.

"Me too," Maggie replied in a breathy whisper, trying not to look at Selene.

There was a short pause, then Clint chuckled. "I get it. Not alone, huh?"

"Right."

"Well, I won't keep you. I just called to tell you I won't be able to see you tonight."

"Oh, Clint," Maggie wailed, no longer caring that Selene was listening. "I was hoping we could celebrate tonight. You know, just the two of us."

"Believe me, sweetheart, I'd like nothing better, but I've got this . . . ah . . . business dinner that I had forgotten about. There's no way I can get out of it at this late date."

"You're sure?"

"I'm afraid so," Clint sighed regretfully. "But I'll make it up to you tomorrow night, honey, I promise.

Now that this sponsorship thing is out of the way you and I need to have a long serious talk. So look, I'll give you a call tomorrow and we'll make plans. Okay?"

"Okay," Maggie agreed disconsolately. "I'll talk to you tomorrow."

"Trouble?"

Meeting Selene's inquiring look, Maggie shook her head and smiled grimly. "No. Not really. I guess I'm just feeling sorry for myself because Clint has a business dinner tonight, which means I won't be seeing him."

"In that case, why don't you have dinner with me? We haven't gone out together in ages. It'll be fun."

Maggie opened her mouth to refuse, then thought better of it. She certainly didn't want to spend the evening moping around the house like a lovesick teenager. Determined to shake off her melancholy mood, she gave her friend a bright smile and said, "Great. I'd love to."

"Super! I'll meet you at Rudi's at eight." Gathering her purse and briefcase, Selene swept out of the room on a cloud of Chanel No. 5 before Maggie could change her mind.

Though she had approached the evening with a decided lack of enthusiasm, by eight thirty that evening Maggie, congratulating herself on her adult behavior, was very glad she had accepted Selene's invitation. Freshly showered, perfumed, and dressed in an elegant midnight-blue lace dress with a ruffled-edged plunging neckline, she was sitting in the plush, dimly lit restaurant enjoying pleasant conversation and a delicious meal of shrimp scampi with an old and dear friend. Which was a darned sight better than staying at home licking your imaginary wounds, she told herself severely.

In all truth, she was enjoying herself . . . until her eyes strayed to the dance floor.

". . . of course I'd been telling Henry all along that you—" Suddenly Selene's words cut off in mid-spate, and she reached across the table to grip Maggie's shaking hand. "My God, Maggie! What is it? You look as though you've seen a ghost!"

Drawing her tortured gaze away from the couple on the dance floor, Maggie met her friend's concerned look and shook her head dazedly. Painfully, she sucked a deep gulp of air into her pained lungs. Until that moment she had not realized she had been holding her breath. "Not a ghost," she replied in a wooden monotone, once again letting her eyes stray toward the dance floor. "Just another two-timing snake."

Stunned by the lashing bitterness in the quiet words, Selene turned in her chair to follow the direction of Maggie's gaze, stiffening when her eyes found the source of her friend's distress. There on the dance floor with a beautiful young woman cradled in his arms was Clint.

Chapter Nine

"Oh, Maggie, love, I'm so sorry."

The music ended, and wide blue eyes, shimmering with pain, watched Clint and his date return to their table on the other side of the dance floor. With an effort of will Maggie pulled her gaze away from the pair and refocused on Selene. The compassion in her friend's expression was almost her undoing, and Maggie had to bite her lower lip to keep it from quivering. Her heart felt like an aching knot in her chest. Her throat was so painfully tight she didn't seem to be able to breathe or swallow. Mutely, she stared at the older woman, unable to say a word.

Holding Maggie's trembling, icy cold hands between her own, Selene made a quick visual reconnaissance of the room before leaning forward and whispering urgently, "Look, Maggie, if we move calmly and keep to the shadows we can make it to the door without being seen. Come on, honey," she urged, squeezing Maggie's hand. "Let's get out of here."

The words brought Maggie's chin up. She drew in a deep, shuddering breath and sat up straighter in her chair, pride overcoming her pain. "No. I'm not going anywhere," she stated in a tone that rang with determination despite its slight quaver. "Especially not just because Clint Rafferty happens to be here with one of his young bimbos." Giving Selene a tight smile, she picked up her fork. "Besides, I haven't finished my dinner yet."

Surprise, admiration, and concern flickered across Selene's face as she stared back at Maggie. After a moment she opened her mouth to argue, but the quick narrowing of Maggie's blue eyes squelched the words before they were uttered. With a sigh and a shrug, Selene picked up her own fork. "Okay. If that's what you want."

What Maggie wanted was to march over there and give Clint a hard poke in the eye, then go somewhere and have a good bawl . . . but she wouldn't. Not only because she wasn't about to let him know how much he had hurt her but because she'd be *damned* if she'd shed another tear over yet another worthless male.

Very calmly, with every outward sign of enjoyment, Maggie speared a succulent shrimp, lifted it to her mouth and chewed slowly. When she swallowed, it felt like ground glass going down her throat. Maggie took a sip of cooling white wine and smiled at Selene.

Damn you, Clint! she raged silently, deliberately whipping up her anger. How dare you do this to me! You and your tender words and your empty promises. They're just so much hot air! And you, Maggie Trent! What a prize fool you are for believing him. You *knew* what kind of man he was! The evidence was right there from the very beginning, as plain as day. But did you listen to your head? No. Of course not. You had to go and fall for the louse so he could cut out your heart and serve it to you on a platter. What are you? Some kind of masochist?

With dogged determination Maggie worked her way through the delicious meal, chewing and swallowing the gourmet food and sipping the fine wine without ever once tasting it, all the while castigating herself mercilessly. Pride and anger were the only weapons she had to keep the terrible pain at bay, and she used them to their fullest.

Finally every morsel was consumed, and the last drop of wine slid down her throat. Delicately, Maggie patted her mouth with her napkin and settled back in her chair with a phony, exaggerated sigh that didn't fool Selene in the least.

"May I ask the waiter for the check now?" the older woman gritted out between tightly clenched teeth.

"Sure. I'm ready whenever you are."

"*I* was ready an hour ago." Selene shot her a harassed look and lifted her hand for the waiter.

When her friend had finished scribbling her name across the check, Maggie picked up her evening bag and rose to her feet, but instead of heading for the door, she turned in the opposite direction.

"Oh, Lord, Maggie!" Selene squeaked. "Where are you going?"

"I'm going to stop by Clint's table and say hello," Maggie tossed over her shoulder, as she began to make her way around the dance floor.

Selene raised her eyes heavenward and groaned. "Of course. How silly of me not to have known." For a moment of sheer helpless frustration she watched Maggie bearing down on her target, then heaved a resigned sigh and rushed after her.

All evening Maggie's gaze had returned over and

over to Clint and his young companion. It was like probing a sore tooth with your tongue—painful but irresistible. She might be hurting, but she wasn't going to hurt alone. No doubt Clint thought he could play these little games without her ever being the wiser, but he was in for a rude awakening.

She was only a few feet from his table when he looked up and saw her, and Maggie felt a sweet surge of satisfaction as she watched his face blanch to a sickly gray.

"Maggie!"

"Hello, Clint. I certainly never expected to run into you here. Life is just chock-full of little surprises, isn't it," she cooed. A pleasant smile curved Maggie's mouth, but her eyes impaled him like icy daggers. "Wasn't it lucky that Selene and I decided to have dinner here tonight?"

Clint jumped awkwardly to his feet, nearly toppling his chair in the process. "Maggie, this isn't what you—"

"Aren't you going to introduce us to your friend?" she interrupted smoothly, before he could complete the stammered excuse.

Clint had the look of a desperate man, his green eyes wide and silently pleading, frustration, anxiety, fear, and wariness all etched in his stricken face. Maggie's answering smile was pure sophistication—cool, meaningless, and withering. The feral gleam in her eyes told him without words that she didn't want to hear anything he had to say.

Briefly, Clint's eyes sought help from Selene, but she merely took a step closer to Maggie and stared back at him as though he were something that had just crawled out from under a rock.

Finally, with a despairing slump of his shoulders, Clint gestured toward the young woman who sat watching them intently. "This is Susan Carstairs. Susan, meet Maggie Trent and Selene Bentley. Maggie is—"

"I produce the television show which Clint and his partner sponsor," Maggie cut in, giving the silent young woman a stiff smile. "Actually, that's why I stopped by your table." Her attention reverted to Clint, and her voice took on a hard, implacable edge. "That meeting we had scheduled for tomorrow is no longer necessary. The entire matter has been cleared up and I've reached a decision . . . and it's irreversible."

"Maggie, you've got to listen to me." Clint reached out for her hand, but Maggie side-stepped him and began to ease away, pulling Selene along with her.

"We won't keep you any longer. Good night, Clint. Ms. Carstairs. Enjoy the rest of your evening."

Head high, face set, Maggie headed toward the exit, swiftly zigzagging her way through the throng of tables, intent only on putting as much space as possible between herself and Clint. Selene was right on her heels. They had barely reached the lobby when he caught up with them.

"Maggie! Wait! You've got to listen to me."

Frigid blue eyes lasered into him. "I don't have to do anything of the kind," she stated cuttingly, slipping her arms into the sleeves of her blue fox jacket and turning for the door.

The space between them was covered in two large strides. Clint grasped her upper arm and spun her around to face him. "Maggie, love, this is not what you obviously think. If you'll just hear me out you'll see that."

Pointedly, Maggie looked down at the big hand sunk deep in the luxuriant fur, then tilted her head back and lifted narrowed eyes to his face. Her softly hissed,

"Take your hands off me," hit him like a spray of fine buckshot, and he released her instantly. The hands at his sides closed into white-knuckled fists. Like a man fast reaching the end of his tether, his face twisted in anguish. "For God's sake, Maggie don't do this to us!" he implored in a low, grating tone. "At least let me explain."

Discreetly, Selene moved away and pretended to study a painting beside the door.

For a brief instant Maggie was struck by the beseeching, almost frightened look on Clint's face, and her heart lurched against her ribcage, but she quickly smothered the weak reaction. She'd had eleven years of protestation and denials and pleas of innocence from Larry. She didn't want to hear anymore. "I'm really not interested." Her eyes scanned the opulent lobby and encountered several curious faces. "And besides, this is hardly the place for explanations of that sort."

Clint sent a scowling look around the room, and most of the gawking patrons squirmed uncomfortably and found something else to look at. "All right. If not now, then later." He flicked back his cuff and shot a quick glance at his watch. "I'll take Susan home and be at your house in half an hour." He turned and took two steps toward the dining room, then stopped and swung back. His face was hard, resolute. "And when I get there you'd better let me in, or so help me, Maggie, I'll kick the door down. We're going to get this thing settled tonight."

Trembling with rage and hurt and a terrible black despair, Maggie watched him walk away. Why was she letting him dictate to her this way? she asked herself bitterly. She should have told him, in no uncertain terms, exactly what he could do with his explanation and been done with it. With a desolate sigh, she dragged her gaze away from his retreating form and walked listlessly toward the door where Selene was waiting. The trouble was, she wanted so badly to believe him. But then, she had wanted to believe Larry, too, and look where it had gotten her.

The thirty minutes gave Maggie time to get herself firmly under control. When she heard Clint's car pull into the drive she was waiting for him, cool and collected, her resolve firm, her face an emotionless mask. The slam of a car door was followed a few seconds later by the heavy thud of steps across the porch. Without waiting for his knock, Maggie opened the door and motioned Clint inside, then turned on her heel and marched into the living room.

In the middle of the floor she swung to face him. Her arms were crossed beneath her breasts. Her eyes were cold and accusing. "You wanted to explain, so explain."

"Can't we sit down."

"No. There's no point. I don't expect this to take long. Just say what you have to say and leave. I'm very tired."

Clint's mouth compressed into a tight line but his voice, when he spoke, was soft and beseeching. "Maggie, I know you're angry and hurt," he began, ignoring the haughty denial in the quick outthrust of her chin. "And I know, from your point of view, I probably look guilty as hell, but believe me, what you saw tonight was perfectly innocent. You see, Susan is Henry Burk's daughter. She's separated from her husband, and she's going through a rough patch right now. Henry told me months ago that she would be coming for a visit during the holidays, and he asked me then if I would take her out while she was in town. I said yes, then promptly forgot about the whole thing. This morning when I arrived at the office he told me that he had taken the liberty of making reservations for us to have dinner tonight at Rudi's." Clint shrugged and spread his hands wide in a helpless, palms-up gesture. "Because she's Henry's daughter, I didn't quite see how I could get out of it gracefully." He paused and waited for her to comment, but Maggie said nothing. Clint sighed and raked a hand through his hair. "Look, I'll admit I handled the entire situation badly, and for that I'm truly sorry. I never meant to hurt or upset you, darling. Surely you know that."

Maggie's expression didn't alter by so much as a twitch. Continuing to stare at him with cold, unfathomable eyes, she neither moved nor made a sound. Her expression was closed. Her silence was ominous.

After a few seconds of expectant waiting Clint could stand it no longer. "For God's sake, Maggie," he burst out. "That's the truth. Honestly!"

"Oh, I believe you," Maggie informed him with an imperious tilt of her head. "But that doesn't change the fact that you lied to me. I had eleven years of lies from a man, and I don't intend to put up with any more."

"But, sweetheart, I didn't lie. I really did look on it as a business commitment," Clint protested earnestly.

Maggie's eyes grew glacial. "But what you neglected to tell me was that your 'business commitment' was a date with your partner's beautiful young daughter. A lie by omission is still a lie."

"Dammit! Did it ever occur to you that I was afraid to tell you? Afraid of just this sort of reaction?" Clint exploded. "Okay, you tell me! Just what would your reaction have been had I explained the situation to you beforehand? Would it have been any different?"

Taken aback by the question, Maggie stared at him blankly for a second before defiantly tossing her hair back over her shoulder and drawing herself up proudly. "Probably not," she admitted.

"Exactly! So do you see why I did what I did? At

least this way I had a chance of getting my obligation out of the way without upsetting you in the process."

"Oh, no you don't! Don't you dare try to put the onus on me or try to pretend you were doing it to protect me," Maggie ground out in a furious voice. Her forefinger stabbed the air in his direction. "What you were doing, whether you want to admit it or not, was trying to have your cake and eat it too! If you had really been thinking of me you would have told Henry that you were no longer free to escort his daughter. The fact that you didn't only proves that it was what you really wanted to do." Smiling cynically, she raked him with a scornful look. "Who knows. If you play your cards right maybe you could even marry the girl. Then someday you'd be the sole owner of the Sporting Chance stores."

The instant she uttered the words, Maggie regretted them. Clint stared at her, his face granite hard, a thin, white line of rage around his compressed mouth.

"I am not in the least interested in acquiring either Henry's share of the business *or* his daughter," he spat out bitterly. "And if you'll recall, you were the one who insisted that we keep our relationship quiet, not me."

Confused, angry, and too distraught even to think, Maggie simply stared back at him, her body quivering in reaction to the tumult of violent emotions surging through her.

Clint eyed her defiant stance and shook his head. "You say you care for me, but you don't trust me. Not one whit. Don't you think I know that? That I can feel it, sense it? Well, let me tell you something, lady, when you really love someone you trust them."

She clasped her arms more tightly against her midriff and lifted her chin. "I don't recall ever telling you that I loved you," she stated haughtily, her voice quivering from the terrible ache in her chest.

Clint looked as though she had slapped him. His eyes were wide and glazed with shock, and muscles worked spasmodically in his cheek. He stared at her for a long, tense moment, then replied quietly, "Well, I guess I misunderstood the situation. Apparently this whole argument has been for nothing." He nodded his head curtly and headed for the door. She barely heard his soft, "Goodbye, Maggie" just before it slammed shut behind him.

In the deafening quiet Maggie could hear her heart pounding against her rib cage. Outside a car door slammed, and seconds later she heard Clint's car roar down the drive and careen away with a squeal of burning rubber. Maggie stood rooted to the spot, staring at the empty doorway, her vision slowly blurring as a wall of tears banked against her lower lids. She looked up at the ceiling and widened her eyes to hold them in check. "I won't cry," she vowed through quivering lips. "I won't."

She trailed across the room to the sofa and curled up in the corner, hugging herself tightly. She stared with sightless eyes at the banked, glowing embers in the fireplace.

Maggie had no idea how long she sat, staring blindly at nothing, but after a while she forced herself to her feet. Mechanically, like someone walking in their sleep, she rechecked the banked fire, snapped off the lamps, and drifted up the stairs in a haze of pain.

Sitting in the darkened car at the curb, Clint watched the lights go out one by one. His large hand curled into a balled fist and struck the steering wheel. He felt so helpless!

He had gone barely a mile when his temper cooled. Impulsively, he had whipped the car around and come back, only realizing the futility of it when he had coasted to a halt in front of her house. What more could he say to her? That he was sorry? He'd already said that, and it hadn't made any difference.

His fist hit the steering wheel again. *Dammit,* this didn't make any sense! She loved him. He knew it, in spite of what she said. It couldn't end like this!

Gripping the wheel tightly with both hands, he let his head sag forward until his chin touched his chest. A low, animal groan forced its way from his throat.

Face it, Rafferty. It not only can, it has. Because love alone isn't enough. You've got to have trust, too. And the lady simply doesn't trust you.

He turned his head and gazed at the house, his eyes going to the upstairs window that still showed a faint glow of lamplight. Gradually, his face hardened.

All right, Maggie. If that's the way you want it, so be it. I'm not your exhusband and if you can't see that for yourself, what's the use?

He pulled his eyes from the lighted window and flicked the ignition key. The smooth purr of the engine barely broke the silence of the night as the car pulled slowly away from the curb.

Maggie glared at Selene over the width of her desk. "*No,* I have not heard from Clint, and *no,* I have not called him, and so help me, if I so much as hear the man's name again I think I'll stand on top of this desk and scream my lungs out!"

"Sorry," Selene drawled, settling back in her chair and blowing a stream of blue smoke toward the ceiling. "Just thought I'd ask."

With a sigh, Maggie propped her elbows on the desk top and dropped her head into her hands, her fingers winnowing through the shining fall of mahogany hair to massage her tight scalp. "No, no. I'm the one who's sorry. I shouldn't have snapped at you like that. It's just that for the past two weeks either Laura or Allison, or sometimes both of them, have been at me constantly. All I hear is how miserable Clint is. How he hasn't been out with anyone else since we broke up. How I ought to give him another chance . . . and so on, and so on, and so on."

Maggie lifted her head and tossed her hair back away from her face. The silky mane immediately settled into its smooth bell shape. "I knew this would happen!" she ranted, striking the desk top with one small fist. "Laura and Allison are both devastated by the break-up. Poor darlings, they had their hopes so high that something permanent would come out of the relationship, and now they're miserable."

"And what about you?" Selene asked quietly. "How are you holding up?"

"Me?" Maggie gave an elaborately casual shrug. "Why I'm just fine." That is, if you called not being able to eat or sleep fine. Or if you didn't count the fact that she couldn't seem to go five minutes without thinking about Clint, and wanted to cry whenever she did, then, yes, she was fine.

"Good. I'm glad to hear it. I wish I could say the same for Clint."

Maggie's head snapped up. "What's that supposed to mean?"

"Only that the girls are right. Clint is miserable. He looks like hell, and he's working himself and everyone around him into the ground. And if that's not bad enough, his disposition makes the Hulk look like a pussycat. Everyone at Sporting Chance and the agency dives for cover when they see him coming." Selene gave Maggie a long, intense look that made her squirm. "Are you really sure you did the right thing, Maggie?

Don't you think that maybe . . . just maybe . . . you may have misjudged the man?"

Resentment, uncertainty, and longing warred within Maggie. It was a battle that had been raging for two weeks. A thousand times she had asked herself if she had been wrong, if she had let the accumulated bitterness and anger of her marriage blind her to the truth, if she had prejudged him simply because, like Larry, he had been an athlete. And a thousand times the answer was the same: she didn't know. As unflattering to herself as the idea was, Maggie wanted to believe it was true. She loved Clint. And she missed him so badly there were times when she didn't think she could get through another day without him. Yet one thing was irrefutable; he *had* lied to her.

She looked at Selene with overbright eyes, all her ambivalent feelings plain on her face. "I . . . I just don't know, I—"

Her stammered reply was cut off when the door to her office was thrust open with such force it crashed against the wall. Both Maggie and Selene looked up in astonishment just as Clint came storming in.

His blazing eyes fixed on Maggie, he strode across to her desk, planted both fists on its top, and leaning forward, snarled, "Get your coat. You're coming with me."

"What?" Maggie's startled eyes grew even wider, then indignation took over. "I most certainly am not," she huffed.

"Just shut up and read this," Clint commanded, slapping a crumpled sheet of paper down on her desk. "And after you've read it, then you can get your coat."

Maggie opened her mouth to argue, but a second look at his face changed her mind. He looked ready to tear something—or someone—in two. Gingerly, she picked up the paper and smoothed it out with her palm.

Then, after one last wary glance at the furious man looming over her, she lowered her eyes and began to read.

"Oh, no!" Maggie looked up at Clint after scanning only the first line, then quickly looked down again. Her eyes raced across the crumpled paper in growing desperation. "No. No! Oh, my God, no!" she cried, unconsciously shaking her head.

"Maggie, love, what is it?" Selene questioned urgently.

Maggie neither heard nor replied. When she raised her head her face was chalk white, and once again her eyes sought Clint's, a frantic plea shimmering in their blue depths. "But . . . but . . . this can't be true," she cried in a voice that verged on hysteria. "This . . . this says—"

"That's right," Clint rapped out harshly. "Allison and Laura have run away."

Chapter Ten

The monochromatic landscape stretched out endlessly on either side of the wide, divided highway, the gently undulating hills covered with a golden brown stubble of winter-dried grass and dotted only here and there with a gnarled, bare tree or a small pond. Occasionally a few cattle could be seen lazily foraging the winter pastures, but most were hidden from view by the gentle rise and fall of the land. The December sky was a washed out color, somewhere between blue and gray, that made a fitting backdrop for the somber scene.

During the past few hours, as they had driven steadily northward, the scenery had gradually changed from the flat sprawling metropolis that was Houston to dense, hilly forest land and finally to these gentle swells that marked the beginning of the prairie. Each was beautiful in its own way, but Maggie had seen none of it. Restlessly, her fingers twisted together in her lap while her eyes frantically searched the side of the highway ahead.

"Are you sure we've taken the right road?" she asked Clint worriedly.

"As sure as I can be. *If,* like their note says, they really are going to my mother's, and *if* those two have a brain between them, then this is the way they would go. Highway 45 is the most direct route between Houston and Dallas."

A low moan escaped Maggie. "Hitchhiking! I can't believe they could be so foolish as to hitchhike!" Fear clawed at her. "Oh, Lord, Clint, anything could have happened to them. Anything!" The last was said on a rising sob as hysteria rose up in her like a flood tide. Maggie clamped her hand over her mouth and took several deep breaths, blinking her eyes furiously as she struggled for control. Since reading that note she had been in the grip of an icy terror, her mind filled with all the horrible things she'd ever read about what happens to young girls who hitchhike. A violent shudder rippled through Maggie, and she wrapped both arms tightly around her midriff. She couldn't let herself think that way. She couldn't!

A hard, warm hand cupped her shoulder and massaged gently. "Don't get yourself worked up so, Maggie. We'll find them. I promise you."

She turned her head and looked at Clint with anguished, tear-filled eyes. The steady determination in his ruggedly handsome face eased the constriction in her chest ever so slightly, and Maggie placed her hand on top of his and gave it a gentle pat. "I know, Clint," she whispered unsteadily. "I know."

"We'll stop up here and call again," Clint said decisively, pointing toward the overhead freeway sign that read "Corsicana Next Exit."

A weak, grateful smile quivered around Maggie's

mouth, but she said nothing. These frequent stops to call ahead and find out if the girls had arrived at Mrs. Rafferty's were slowing them down, but neither she nor Clint could stand the suspense of not knowing. So far they had stopped at Conroe, Huntsville, Centerville, and Fairfield, all with the same results: Clint's mother had not heard a word from Allison and Laura. Yet when Clint took the exit ramp and swung the car into the service station at the freeway intersection, Maggie felt hope rise inside her again.

"Be right back," Clint said distractedly as he climbed from the car and slammed the door behind him. He strode over to the telephone booth, stepped inside, and pulled the folding door closed behind him.

Her nerves drawn taut as a bow string, Maggie watched his every move, unconsciously digging her fingernails deep into the plush velour seat on either side of her. The minutes seemed to drag by. She couldn't see Clint's face clearly, but when he slammed the receiver back onto the hook and nearly tore the folding door from its hinges getting it open she knew, and her shoulders slumped.

"Still no word," he clipped out in mounting frustration when he slipped back behind the wheel. He cast a quick, concerned look at Maggie's strained face, then sent the car roaring back onto the road.

Lost in their own thoughts, both Clint and Maggie remained silent as the powerful car ate up the miles. At any other time Maggie would have been terrified of driving so fast, but now she was too preoccupied with other fears. They were rapidly coming to the end of their trip. There were only two towns between them and Dallas. Maggie knew that with each passing mile their chances of catching up to the girls grew slimmer and slimmer.

A shudder shook Maggie's slight frame, and she

hugged herself tighter. In their note Allison and Laura had said they were going to spend Christmas with Allison's grandmother because they couldn't stand the hostility between their parents any longer, and since reading it Maggie had been consumed with guilt. She had known the girls were upset over the break-up, but she hadn't realized they were upset enough to run away. She cast a sidelong glance at Clint through her lashes. Was this whole mess her fault? Had she been wrong not to trust him? Wrong not to give him a second chance? She honestly didn't know. All she was sure of at the moment was that she was terribly grateful he was here with her. She didn't think she could bear this ordeal alone.

At the next town Clint again pulled off the freeway and sought the nearest phone, and again Maggie waited in the car, her nerves screaming. But this time when he tore out of the booth his face was lit up like a Christmas tree. Maggie's heart leaped up into her throat and hung there as she watched him stride to the car and yank the door open.

"They're there, Maggie!" Clint slid onto the seat and reached for her all in one motion. He hauled her onto his lap and hugged her tightly to his chest. "They're okay. They're safe," he murmured shakily against her hair. "They arrived at Mother's just minutes after my last call." He buried his face against the side of her neck, and Maggie could feel the tremors that rippled through his big body. She knew that they were echoed in her own.

"Oh, thank God," were the only words she managed to utter before bursting into tears. Relief washed through her, draining her of every ounce of strength. Weakly Maggie clung to Clint and sobbed out all the pent-up anguish and fear that had been bottled up inside her, her shoulders shaking with each wrenching cry. Within minutes her tears had soaked his soft flannel shirt. The feel of his strong arms holding her close was the most comforting thing in the world, and Maggie lay against him like a ragdoll and wailed her profound relief, her face buried against his warm, muscular chest.

Clint held her close and rocked her back and forth, his big hands stroking and caressing her back and shoulders as he crooned soothing words in her ear. They were oblivious to the traffic streaming by and the curious stares they were receiving from the other people at the service station.

After a few minutes the worst of the storm was over, but when Maggie would have pulled away Clint tightened his hold. "It's all right, sweetheart," he reassured her softly. Her sobs had dwindled to a series of shuddering sighs, and he cradled her close as though to absorb them into his own body. She could feel his warm breath filtering through her hair to caress her scalp as he pressed tender kisses against her temple. Maggie shivered and rubbed her cheek against his chest.

"I've missed you so, darling," Clint whispered. "I thought I'd go crazy with missing you."

Maggie wanted to reply that she had missed him too, but the words could not get past her aching throat.

"Maggie, love," Clint began softly, hesitantly. "I didn't lie to you, sweetheart. I really did think of that dinner with Susan as a business commitment. I'd never be unfaithful to you, darling. You've got to believe me."

Slowly, Maggie raised her head, her shimmering, tear-drenched eyes awash with feeling as they searched his face. Suddenly, as she stared at the heart-wrenching longing and near despair in his expression, all her doubts disappeared, all her anger and worries and fears slipped away into nothingness. A tremulous smile curved her mouth, and she lifted her hand to tenderly cup his strong jaw. "I do believe you, darling," she whispered.

Clint sucked in his breath, and a flame leaped to life in his eyes. "Oh, Lord, Maggie! You don't know what it means to me to hear you say that," he groaned hoarsely as he lowered his mouth to hers.

The kiss was long and soft and infinitely sweet. Maggie felt as though her soul had suddenly taken fire. With delicious languor and hesitancy, lips, hands, and bodies became reacquainted. And when it was over they simply clung together in shared relief and happiness, neither saying a word for several minutes.

When at last Clint sat her away from him, he pulled a clean handkerchief from his pocket and tenderly mopped Maggie's tear-streaked face. "I love you, Maggie," he whispered, and Maggie's breath caught in her throat as joy streaked through her.

"I love you, too," she replied shakily.

Clint's eyes flared briefly, then he bent his head and placed a swift, hard kiss on her mouth. "You and I need to have a long talk," he informed her with a gentle smile. "But I'm afraid it will have to wait until we've dealt with our daughters."

Maggie straightened her clothing and combed shaky fingers through her hair. "Yes, you're right," she agreed, then shuddered delicately. "Sweet heaven, when I think of the risk they took my blood runs cold."

Clint's face became suddenly hard. Abruptly, he flicked the ignition and put the car in gear. "Not as much as you think," he said sharply. "It seems the little dears took the bus."

"The bus? Do you mean to tell me I've been worrying myself sick and all the while those two were on a bus?"

"That's about the size of it."

Maggie made a low sound deep in her throat and flounced around in her seat. "Just you wait until I get my hands on those two. I'm going to wring their necks!"

"I'm afraid you'll have to wait in line," Clint growled ominously and pushed the gas pedal to the floor.

It was almost dark when they pulled into the driveway beside Mrs. Rafferty's neat, brick home. She had obviously been looking for them, for before Clint could ring the bell she opened the door and motioned them inside.

"Where are they?" he demanded uncivilly, before his mother could say a word.

Emma Rafferty wasn't in the least intimidated. Folding her arms under her ample bosom, she met her son's hard glare with unblinking directness. She was a big, raw-boned woman, only four or five inches under Clint's impressive height. Standing between them, Maggie felt like a Lilliputian.

"Now just hold on there," Mrs. Rafferty commanded, her lined, strong-boned face stern. "Before you go off half-cocked, I think you should know that Allison and Laura only pulled this stunt in the hope of getting the two of you back together." Pointedly, she looked down at Maggie and Clint's joined hands, and a small smile softened her mouth. "And from the looks of things, I'd say they succeeded. I'd think the two of you would be grateful, not angry."

"After the scare they gave us?" Clint demanded incredulously. "You *can't* be serious!"

"And what about the scare you gave them?" his mother countered. "Those girls were convinced that if they didn't take a hand in matters the two of you would never speak to one another again." She paused long enough to shoot Maggie a quick look. "By the way, I'm Emma Rafferty, this lout's mother."

"How do you do, Mrs. Rafferty," Maggie replied quickly. "I'm terribly sorry about all this, and for barging in on you this way."

"Don't give it a thought." She dismissed Maggie's apology with an airy wave of her hand, then subjected her to a slow appraisal. "You're a little bitty thing, but from what I hear from my granddaughter I'd say you're a good match for my son. It's high time he settled down with a decent woman."

Maggie felt a blush start at the base of her neck and spread all the way up to her hairline. She was so embarrassed she couldn't think of a single thing to say, which was just as well because Emma Rafferty's attention had already swung back to her son.

"Now I want your promise that you won't be too hard on those girls when I call them out here, Clint," she admonished sternly. "After all, they had your best interest at heart, and no harm came to them."

"Mother!" Clint clipped in exasperation. "Don't you see—"

"Your word, Clint." Emma tilted her strong jaw aggressively. Her short, gray curls shone like polished silver under the foyer light. Her dark eyes glittered like black shoe buttons. Watching this formidable woman, Maggie knew exactly where Clint got both his looks and his determination.

"Oh, all right," he relented sourly. "I won't chew them up and spit them out for dogmeat, if that's what you mean."

"Not exactly, but it will do for now," Emma said, moving toward the door at the back of the hall. "You two go on into the living room. I'll send them in."

A few minutes later, each holding tightly to the other's hand, their faces stricken with guilt and apprehension, Allison and Laura edged reluctantly into the room where their parents stood waiting. Emma Rafferty was right behind them.

At the first sight of her daughter all the anger drained out of Maggie and she stepped forward, enfolding Laura in a tight embrace. After only the barest hesitation, Clint pulled his own daughter to him. Standing to one side, Emma Rafferty viewed the emotional scene with a warm smile and suspiciously moist eyes.

Finally Clint and Maggie released the girls and stepped back. Clint cleared his throat. Fixing first one girl then the other with a stern look, he growled, "Well? What have you two got to say for yourselves?"

Laura shifted her weight from one foot to the other and stared down at the floor.

Allison looked to her grandmother for support, then gamely met her father's eyes. "We're sorry that we worried you like that, but we *had* to do something. It's perfectly obvious that you two belong together, but you're both just so darned stubborn." She shook her head and sighed disgustedly. "You were both miserable, but neither one of you would make the first move, so we decided to give you a little help."

Clint tried to keep a stern expression but his daughter's audacity proved too much for him. Reluctantly, his mouth curved upward at the corners. He looked down at Maggie and shook his head, then hooked an arm around her waist and brought her up close against his side before returning his attention to Allison and Laura. "Luckily for you two, things worked out just fine this time. But do me a favor. The next time you decide to help us . . . don't."

"You're a terrible man, Clinton Rafferty," Maggie breathed huskily against the side of Clint's neck. Her lips nibbled delicately at the brown skin as though savoring a delicious treat, while her fingers worked at his shirt button with tantalizing slowness. "Scandalous, really."

"Um hmmmm," he agreed with blatant male satisfaction.

"First you rush us out of your mother's house so quickly we barely had time to eat breakfast or say goodbye, then we no sooner get home than you get rid of the girls and drag me to the couch." She nipped gently at his earlobe. "You really are awful."

"I wanted you to myself for a while, that's all," he informed her as his hands ran boldly over her curves.

"But don't you think you were being just a bit obvious when you whipped out a fist full of money and sent the girls off to the movies? Whatever will they think?"

"That I'm about to make love to you, probably," he answered with lazy unconcern, releasing the buttons on her blouse one by one. "And they'll be right." The red silk blouse was pushed over her shoulders and quickly disposed of as Clint eased Maggie down onto the sofa cushions. Bracing up on his elbows, he smiled down into her bemused face. "But before we get to that I think it's time we talked about the future," he rumbled softly, and Maggie's heart took off like a runaway locomotive. Caressing her with his eyes, he whispered, "I love you, Maggie, and I want you for my wife."

Devilishly, Maggie pursed her lips as though mulling it over, and Clint's eyes narrowed.

"Say yes, you little wretch!"

"Yes, you little wretch," she parroted with a grin.

Clint groaned. "Maggie, so help me . . ."

His protest was cut off as Maggie linked her fingers behind his neck and brought his head down to hers. When their lips met she moaned softly as sweet waves of desire began to lap over her. Maggie reveled in the feel of his heavy masculine body, pressing her deep into the soft cushions, the hot thrust of his tongue filling her mouth, the musky, maleness that assailed her senses like an aphrodisiac. Clint was hers and she was his, and nothing else mattered.

Clint felt Maggie's small hands flutter over his shoulders and drift down his back, and he moaned softly, his heart soaring. He was in heaven, he was sure of it.

Then, without warning, something wet and warm rasped over the back of his neck, breaking the sensual spell as effectively as a douse of cold water.

"What the—Tiny! You idiot animal!" Clint roared, shoving the black-muzzled face away from his neck. "Get away from me! And cut out that giggling, you little devil!"

Whining pathetically and deeply hurt by his hero's sharp rejection, Tiny scurried to the hearth. After a couple of experimental circles, he lowered his big body to the rug and lay his snout on his crossed paws. The soft, rustling sounds and murmured words of love issuing from the sofa drew his attention, and for a moment he gazed dolefully at the entwined couple, then, with a long sigh, discreetly turned his head and went to sleep.

Genuine Silhouette
sterling silver bookmark
for only $15.95!

What a beautiful way to hold your place in your current romance! This genuine sterling silver bookmark, with the

distinctive Silhouette symbol in elegant black, measures 1½″ long and 1″ wide. It makes a beautiful gift for yourself, and for every romantic you know! And, at only $15.95 each, including all postage and handling charges, you'll want to order several now, while supplies last.

Send your name and address with check or money order for $15.95 per bookmark ordered to
Simon & Schuster Enterprises
120 Brighton Rd., P.O. Box 5020
Clifton, N.J. 07012
Attn: Bookmark

Bookmarks can be ordered pre-paid only. No charges will be accepted. Please allow 4-6 weeks for delivery.

Silhouette Romance

IT'S YOUR OWN SPECIAL TIME
Contemporary romances for today's women.
Each month, six very special love stories will be yours
from SILHOUETTE.

$1.75 each

☐ 100 Stanford	☐ 128 Hampson	☐ 157 Vitek	☐ 185 Hampson
☐ 101 Hardy	☐ 129 Converse	☐ 158 Reynolds	☐ 186 Howard
☐ 102 Hastings	☐ 130 Hardy	☐ 159 Tracy	☐ 187 Scott
☐ 103 Cork	☐ 131 Stanford	☐ 160 Hampson	☐ 188 Cork
☐ 104 Vitek	☐ 132 Wisdom	☐ 161 Trent	☐ 189 Stephens
☐ 105 Eden	☐ 133 Rowe	☐ 162 Ashby	☐ 190 Hampson
☐ 106 Dailey	☐ 134 Charles	☐ 163 Roberts	☐ 191 Browning
☐ 107 Bright	☐ 135 Logan	☐ 164 Browning	☐ 192 John
☐ 108 Hampson	☐ 136 Hampson	☐ 165 Young	☐ 193 Trent
☐ 109 Vernon	☐ 137 Hunter	☐ 166 Wisdom	☐ 194 Barry
☐ 110 Trent	☐ 138 Wilson	☐ 167 Hunter	☐ 195 Dailey
☐ 111 South	☐ 139 Vitek	☐ 168 Carr	☐ 196 Hampson
☐ 112 Stanford	☐ 140 Erskine	☐ 169 Scott	☐ 197 Summers
☐ 113 Browning	☐ 142 Browning	☐ 170 Ripy	☐ 198 Hunter
☐ 114 Michaels	☐ 143 Roberts	☐ 171 Hill	☐ 199 Roberts
☐ 115 John	☐ 144 Goforth	☐ 172 Browning	☐ 200 Lloyd
☐ 116 Lindley	☐ 145 Hope	☐ 173 Camp	☐ 201 Starr
☐ 117 Scott	☐ 146 Michaels	☐ 174 Sinclair	☐ 202 Hampson
☐ 118 Dailey	☐ 147 Hampson	☐ 175 Jarrett	☐ 203 Browning
☐ 119 Hampson	☐ 148 Cork	☐ 176 Vitek	☐ 204 Carroll
☐ 120 Carroll	☐ 149 Saunders	☐ 177 Dailey	☐ 205 Maxam
☐ 121 Langan	☐ 150 Major	☐ 178 Hampson	☐ 206 Manning
☐ 122 Scofield	☐ 151 Hampson	☐ 179 Beckman	☐ 207 Windham
☐ 123 Sinclair	☐ 152 Halston	☐ 180 Roberts	☐ 208 Halston
☐ 124 Beckman	☐ 153 Dailey	☐ 181 Terrill	☐ 209 LaDame
☐ 125 Bright	☐ 154 Beckman	☐ 182 Clay	☐ 210 Eden
☐ 126 St. George	☐ 155 Hampson	☐ 183 Stanley	☐ 211 Walters
☐ 127 Roberts	☐ 156 Sawyer	☐ 184 Hardy	☐ 212 Young

$1.95 each

☐ 213 Dailey	☐ 217 Vitek	☐ 221 Browning	☐ 225 St. George
☐ 214 Hampson	☐ 218 Hunter	☐ 222 Carroll	☐ 226 Hampson
☐ 215 Roberts	☐ 219 Cork	☐ 223 Summers	☐ 227 Beckman
☐ 216 Saunders	☐ 220 Hampson	☐ 224 Langan	☐ 228 King

Silhouette Romance

$1.95 each

☐ 229 Thornton	☐ 253 James	☐ 277 Wilson	☐ 301 Palmer
☐ 230 Stevens	☐ 254 Palmer	☐ 278 Hunter	☐ 302 Smith
☐ 231 Dailey	☐ 255 Smith	☐ 279 Ashby	☐ 303 Langan
☐ 232 Hampson	☐ 256 Hampson	☐ 280 Roberts	☐ 304 Cork
☐ 233 Vernon	☐ 257 Hunter	☐ 281 Lovan	☐ 305 Browning
☐ 234 Smith	☐ 258 Ashby	☐ 282 Halldorson	☐ 306 Gordon
☐ 235 James	☐ 259 English	☐ 283 Payne	☐ 307 Wildman
☐ 236 Maxam	☐ 260 Martin	☐ 284 Young	☐ 308 Young
☐ 237 Wilson	☐ 261 Saunders	☐ 285 Gray	☐ 309 Hardy
☐ 238 Cork	☐ 262 John	☐ 286 Cork	☐ 310 Hunter
☐ 239 McKay	☐ 263 Wilson	☐ 287 Joyce	☐ 311 Gray
☐ 240 Hunter	☐ 264 Vine	☐ 288 Smith	☐ 312 Vernon
☐ 241 Wisdom	☐ 265 Adams	☐ 289 Saunders	☐ 313 Rainville
☐ 242 Brooke	☐ 266 Trent	☐ 290 Hunter	☐ 314 Palmer
☐ 243 Saunders	☐ 267 Chase	☐ 291 McKay	☐ 315 Smith
☐ 244 Sinclair	☐ 268 Hunter	☐ 292 Browning	
☐ 245 Trent	☐ 269 Smith	☐ 293 Morgan	
☐ 246 Carroll	☐ 270 Camp	☐ 294 Cockcroft	
☐ 247 Halldorson	☐ 271 Allison	☐ 295 Vernon	
☐ 248 St. George	☐ 272 Forrest	☐ 296 Paige	
☐ 249 Scofield	☐ 273 Beckman	☐ 297 Young	
☐ 250 Hampson	☐ 274 Roberts	☐ 298 Hunter	
☐ 251 Wilson	☐ 275 Browning	☐ 299 Roberts	
☐ 252 Roberts	☐ 276 Vernon	☐ 300 Stephens	

SILHOUETTE BOOKS, Department SB/1

1230 Avenue of the Americas
New York, NY 10020

Please send me the books I have checked above. I am enclosing $_____
(please add 75¢ to cover postage and handling. NYS and NYC residents please
add appropriate sales tax). Send check or money order—no cash or C.O.D.'s
please. Allow six weeks for delivery.

NAME _____

ADDRESS _____

CITY _____ STATE/ZIP _____

MAIL THIS COUPON
and get 4 thrilling

Silhouette Desire®

novels <u>FREE</u> (a $7.80 value)

Silhouette Desire books may not be for everyone. They *are* for readers who want a sensual, provocative romance. These are modern love stories that are charged with emotion from the first page to the thrilling happy ending—about women who discover the extremes of fiery passion. Confident women who face the challenge of today's world and overcome all obstacles to attain their dreams—*and their desires.*

We believe you'll be so delighted with Silhouette Desire romance novels that you'll want to receive them regularly through our home subscription service. Your books will be *shipped to you two months before they're available anywhere else*—so you'll never miss a new title. Each month we'll send you 6 new books to look over for 15 days, without obligation. If not delighted, simply return them and owe nothing. Or keep them and pay only $1.95 each. There's no charge for postage or handling. And there's no obligation to buy anything at any time. You'll also receive a subscription to the Silhouette Books Newsletter *absolutely free!*

So don't wait. To receive your four FREE books, fill out and mail the coupon below *today!*

SILHOUETTE DESIRE and colophon are registered trademarks and a service mark of Simon & Schuster. Inc

---

Silhouette Desire® 120 Brighton Road, P.O. Box 5020, Clifton, NJ 07015

Yes, please send me FREE and without obligation, 4 exciting Silhouette Desire books. Unless you hear from me after I receive them, send me 6 new Silhouette Desire books to preview each month before they're available anywhere else. I understand that you will bill me just $1.95 each for a total of $11.70—with no additional shipping, handling or other hidden charges. **There is no minimum number of books that I must buy, and I can cancel anytime I wish.** The first 4 books are mine to keep, even if I never take a single additional book.

☐ Mrs. ☐ Miss ☐ Ms. ☐ Mr.   **BDR8R4**

Name _____ *(please print)* _____

Address _____ Apt. # _____

City _____ State _____ Zip _____

(___) _____
Area Code   Telephone Number

Signature (If under 18, parent or guardian must sign.) _____

This offer, limited to one per household, expires February 28, 1985. Terms and prices are subject to change. Your enrollment is subject to acceptance by Simon & Schuster Enterprises.

READERS' COMMENTS ON SILHOUETTE ROMANCES:

"The best time of my day is when I put my children to bed at naptime and sit down to read a Silhouette Romance. Keep up the good work."

P.M.*, Allegan, MI

"I am very fond of the quality of your Silhouette Romances. They are so real. I have tried to read some of the other romances, but I always come back to Silhouette."

C.S., Mechanicsburg, PA

"I feel that Silhouette Books offer a wider choice and/or variety than any of the other romance books available."

R.R., Aberdeen, WA

"I have enjoyed reading Silhouette Romances for many years now. They are light and refreshing. You can always put yourself in the main characters' place, feeling alive and beautiful."

J.M.K., San Antonio, TX

"My boyfriend always teases me about Silhouette Books. He asks me, how's my love life and naturally I say terrific, but I tell him that there is always room for a little more romance from Silhouette."

F.N., Ontario, Canada

*names available on request